Eliza Keary

Memoir of Annie Keary

Eliza Keary

Memoir of Annie Keary

ISBN/EAN: 9783337093983

Printed in Europe, USA, Canada, Australia, Japan

Cover: Foto ©Raphael Reischuk / pixelio.de

More available books at **www.hansebooks.com**

MEMOIR

OF

ANNIE KEARY

By HER SISTER

"Rose leaves, when the rose is dead,
Are heaped for the belovèd's bed ;
And so thy thoughts, when thou art gone,
Love itself shall slumber on."

London

MACMILLAN AND CO

1882.

MEMOIR

OF

ANNIE KEARY

MEMOIR

ERRATA.

Page 2, line 23, *delete* "back."
  ,,   3, ,, 26, *for* "first and self," *read* "self and first."
  ,,   3, ,, 27, *delete* "comma," *after* "opening."
  ,, 49, ,, 31, *for* "sunshine," *read* "beauty."
  ,, 52, ,, 23, *for* "teaching," *read* "teachings."
  ,, 55, ,,   5, *for* "Bourdillon," *read* "Papillon."
  ,, 55, ,, 19, *delete* "at first."
  ,, 57, ,, 22, *for* "when," *read* "that."
  ,, 62, ,, 14, *for* "bent," *read* "best."
  ,, 67, ,, 23, *insert* "comma," *after* "which."
  ,, 67, ,, 30, *insert* "of," *after* "this."
  ,, 69, ,, 20, *insert* "commas," *after* "think and signs."
  ,, 72, ,, 13, *for* "scenal," *read* "scenic."
  ,, 86, ,, 10, *delete* "of," *after* "taking a room."
  ,, 89, ,,   1, *delete* "of," *after* "seeing."
  ,, 92, ,, 15, *for* "flat bread cakes," *read* "flat loaves of bread."
  ,, 107, ,, 12, *for* "the man we call," *read* "a man we call."
  ,, 112, ,,   1, *for* "Rhamses," *read* "Ramses."
  ,, 131, ,, 22, *for* "unaltered," *read* "altered."

her works. I must premise that her life was a very quiet one, almost uneventful; the task before me is indeed rather to trace the growth of a character than to give the record of a life. I invite my readers to walk step by step with the subject of

B

MEMOIR

OF

ANNIE KEARY.

PART I.

" I WISH her gentle life were written. Her works are not the full expression of herself; no written thing could express all the wealth of her gracious womanhood, and sweet human-heartedness." These words, which appeared in a notice of Annie Keary's writings in the pages of *Macmillan's Magazine*, and the wishes of many friends who have said to me, " You ought to tell us something more about her," have made me consider whether there might not be something that I ought to say, some simple record that I might make, which would give pleasure to those who knew Annie Keary personally, as well as to those who have known her heretofore only through her works. I must premise that her life was a very quiet one, almost uneventful; the task before me is indeed rather to trace the growth of a character than to give the record of a life. I invite my readers to walk step by step with the subject of

B

these pages; from gracious childhood, through peaceful useful prime, up to the sudden opening of that
gate through which she passed from mortal sight.
Perhaps some soothing influence may flow out upon
us in this contact with one of a gentle, unworldly
nature. If it should seem to some that we linger
unduly over the picture of Annie's early childhood, I
would ask them to recall how much they *lived* in
those days when every sensation was new to them,
and to take account of the moulding power which
the impressions of childhood have had upon them.

Of the persons and things that surrounded Annie
I wish to speak in their action upon her life, therefore any detailed description of them in their relation
to others is unnecessary. A few words will suffice
to introduce her family and parents. Annie's father
was William Keary, the only son of an Irish gentleman, of Clough, near Tuam, in the county of Galway.
Her mother was Lucy, the fifth daughter of Hall
Plumer, Esq., of Bilton Hall, near Wetherby, in
Yorkshire. Mr. Keary entered the army very early
in life, and served through the greater part of the
Peninsular war. He came back to England from the
Continent when he was twenty-three, and married.
Shortly after, on account of an entire change in his
prospects from the loss of his property in Ireland, he
was forced to sell out of the army. He then settled
in England, and in the course of a year or two he
took holy orders. He was appointed to the living of
Bilton, and afterwards to the perpetual curacy of
Sculcoates, a part of the town of Hull, with which

preferment he also held the small living of Nunnington in the North Riding of Yorkshire. Annie's
father was a man of great power of mind, and of
intellectual tastes, a patient student of theology, and
the author of several books upon controversial and
religious subjects. He was an eloquent preacher,
and, as a parish clergyman, he is still remembered
with love and reverence in the places where he
lived and worked. In all his labour amongst the
poor he had the help and sympathy of his wife,
who, almost equally with himself, was looked up to
and valued by his parishioners. During a consider-
able portion of his later life he was unfortunately
debarred by great physical suffering from undertaking either active duty or literary work, or from
in any way making his influence publicly felt.

At the time of Annie's birth her father was the
rector of Bilton, her mother's own early home, and it
was there, on the 3rd of March, 1825—a genial third
of March as it chanced to be that year, when snowdrops and violets were making glad the nooks of the
rector's quiet garden—that Annie Keary was born,
being the sixth child in a family which already
numbered four sons and one daughter. One can
fancy how she might have pictured her surroundings
in after years, looking back to the small first self
opening, loving, wondering eyes upon the home. At
once the young spirit, could it have been conscious
of such things, would have recognised the materials
out of which many of its joyous fancies were here-
after to be woven. First there was Annie's father,

of whom we have already spoken, and to whom she
was by nature more akin than were any of his other
children. He was somewhat broken in health even
as Annie first remembered him ; gentle, genial, not
very gay tempered, enthusiastically religious, affectionate, sensitive, with all the outward and inward
graces that belong to the best of the Irish race, and
with some of the weaknesses also, but these of such
a nature as only made him the dearer to his children.
Between him and Annie, even the child Annie, there
existed always a tender affection and a full confidence. They understood each other so well, these
two, who represented the Irish side of the family,
who both loved their books so tenderly, who thought
and dreamed, who lived and met in an ideal upper
region, exchanging sweet smiles and confidences
there over the heads of the drudging world below.
There was ever a sort of comradeship between them,
and when Annie was quite a small thing she would
sit upon her father's knee for hours while he told her
stories of his youth ; sometimes it might be of his
wild Irish home, or again of the adventures in his
campaigning career, when as a soldier he had lived
out all the dashing, gay, thoroughly Irish part of him.
"This and this you and I did or dared together,
Nannie," he would then say, humouring a favourite
childish fancy of hers that she had really been his
companion in arms, the comrade of all his early life.
"'Twas you and I held fast side by side through that
stiff march across the common in the heat ; we two
stormed Badajoz together, child ; " and the child, as

her imagination fed greedily upon such congenial food, believed more firmly in the fancy which had originated in her own small brain, and began already to live the two lives of the dreamer, the tale-teller, taking her first lesson in novel-writing at her father's knee. " Yes, yes," she would dream, " it was papa and Annie who fought under Wellington together, and now they sit by the fire in cosy winter evenings, the two old comrades, and live the campaign over again; " or letting her thoughts reach back to some dim, remoter period of existence, would see sweet, misty pictures of the west, hear the soft clatter of the Irish tongue, run barefooted across the bog with merry little foster-brothers and sisters, to fish in the blue mountain lough, or to feast upon sweet milk and potatoes at the foster-parents' board in the cabin where papa was nursed, and where he laughed and sported away so many careless hours—but, somehow, never without Annie, how could he ever have been anywhere without her ?

I have said that the father, though genial, was not gay tempered, as his younger children remember him. The mother could have told of brightness in the days gone by, when they had been young together, and the light-hearted Irish officer had won her heart ; but the mother was reserved concerning her deepest feelings, and she did not often talk of those days to her children. She could draw pictures of her own early life for their amusement though ; of the country home in which she had been so happy in spite of what seemed, to our generation,

the stiffness and sternness of its constitution. How
clearly she made us see her father before whom all
trembled excepting herself, his favourite child, how
well contrasted with his was the fainter portrait of
the lady of the house in the sort of state that surrounded her. Then there were the sisters whose
lives she made us realise by her charming description
of their old-fashioned childhood, with its country
luxuries and amusements, the trim flower gardens,
the perfume distilleries, the toy spinning-wheels.
But better still were the stories that took us to a
generation yet further away, whose scene was laid
in a tumble-down old place called Lilling Hall, where
our mother's grandmother had lived, with the old
maiden aunt of the family, always known by the
name of "Little Aunt Anne." Those were almost
fairy tales our mother told us of the ideal days which
she and her sisters had been wont to pass there
in delicious idleness, when the heaviest burden of
the summer hours consisted in the picking of rose
leaves and lavender for the *pot-pourri* that little
Aunt Anne was so marvellously skilled in making.
I have some of the very stuff by me now, in its
old purple jar, the last relic of Lilling Hall, and
it is still sweet with the scent of a hundred years
ago. Yes, the mother could draw smiling English
landscapes, well ordered and beautiful, upon her
canvas, and portraits too, full of humour, of the
hearty Yorkshire folk whom she remembered,
around whom quaint stories clustered such as we
children loved to listen to, and on the recollection

of which Annie was able to draw in her writings afterwards. I think that her tale-telling power came in a greater degree from the mother than from the father, certainly her fund of humour was drawn wholly from the maternal source, but she inherited imagination from both her parents.

From the parents we turn to the brothers and sisters of the family. What were the young ones like, amongst whom Annie found herself? What were they to *her*, as she began to know them? The relationship between Annie and the very dear eldest brother, who from the height of his greatness was wont to make himself so exquisitely familiar with his much-petted little sister, is pictured in that of Janet to *her* favourite brother in Annie's novel *Janet's Home*, and also in the love that her " little Helen " is made to feel for her big brother Hilary in the story of *Father Phim*. " Hilary used to lift Helen on to his shoulder," the story says, "and carry her up the dark back stairs to the smallest of the lumber rooms, where he kept some tame fish in an old water-butt—' dear old Father Phim,' he would sometimes say, quite softly, using his pet play name for her, as he was carrying her up through the dark, and Helen felt as if she were growing very tall, such a quantity of love swelled up in her heart for Hilary."

This brother, the brother next to him in age (with whose life Annie's was intimately connected in later years), and the sister seven years her senior, stand aside as the elders of the group, for they were passing out of the nursery life as Annie was growing up into it.

The eldest sister well remembers that 3rd of March which gave her first sister to her. More than fifty years afterwards, when on a visit to the old Yorkshire home, she speaks of it thus in a letter written to Annie, then drawing very near to death :—

"How clearly I recalled that bright March morning," she wrote, "when I ran off by myself to this sheltered corner of the dear old shrubbery to look for the earliest violets of the season. It had always been my great pride and delight to bring to our mother the first bunch of violets from the roots that she and her sisters had planted in their happy childish days. How my heart beat with anxiety on that particular day, how my eyes swam with foreboding fear, for it was still rather an early search in that cold northern home. It was the 3rd of March, darling, your birthday, and early in the morning, when Bella the ill-tempered nursery-maid dressed me, she had said in a half-triumphant way several times, 'No more fine times for you, Miss Lucy, mamma won't think nothing of you now; she's got another little daughter a deal prettier than you are. I firmly believed all she said, and I thought that, if added to this new claimant on my mother's love, there should be such a failure on my part as the want of the usual spring nosegay, there could indeed be no further chance for me. How strange it was that I should have received with tears and sad forebodings that which brought me the priceless treasure of a

sister's love, my first precious sister, the first link in
that threefold cord that bound us sisters together in
a bond stronger than death, sweeter and deeper than
any tongue can tell, and such as few hearts can
understand."

Loving words which brought a joy like the joy of
Heaven into the sick room, I remember, for love was
always the very bread of life to Annie's gentle soul.
She had found the nest well lined with it, we see, into
which God laid down her babyhood, and what she
received there she gave out to others a hundredfold.

"We," "we two," expressed the earliest loving
impulse of the child, "you and me," or "all of us
together," but the little hand was oftenest clasped
in comradeship of love and mirth by her brother
Arthur, the next above Annie in age, her first
faithful, untiring playmate. "We'll do what we
think proper," was the favourite game of these little
urchins, a pastime of ever-varying moods accord-
ingly as it originated in one or the other audacious
little brain, but one which never failed to put
to the rout all nursery quiet and decorum, and
greatly to aggravate the temper of strict old Nurse
Bream, the tyrant of the epoch. Nurse Bream
had borne with the elder children; it had been a
hard struggle enough, but "there was not one of
them who ever had inventions such as Master
Arthur and Miss Annie had." Inventions—yes, that
was the key-note. Perhaps Mrs. Bream did not
make sufficient allowance for the circumstances in
which the little ones of the second period were placed

as compared with those enjoyed by the elders. Their romping time had been passed at the dear old Rectory, where they had had the run of field and garden, ponies to ride, pet animals to look after; but all this had been changed before Annie became the clever sprite in whose atmosphere the good nurse's most stringent discipline found itself at once short-sighted and infirm.

Before the time when Annie could remember anything, the family had removed from the little Yorkshire village to Hull, the large, mercantile town, in which a new sphere of work had opened out to the father. The ideal country times were nothing better than a tradition to the younger children therefore, whose pleasures were cruelly circumscribed by the conditions of town life. No roaming about for them just as the fancy took them, no running out of doors at all without hats on. In the house it was not much better. Study and work had to be carried on there; it was necessary that there should be some limit to the noise; the whole world was, in fact, nothing but a dull hole of a place, scarcely big enough to turn round in.

Do not plants bring forth flowers only by reason of checks applied to the wildness of their growth ? Take a handful of lily-of-the-valley roots on some early spring day, and crush them into a small flower-pot, and by and by the flowers will bloom and fill our houses with their fragrance. As it is with the flowers, so it was with the children of whom Annie was one; with them imagination flowered with unwearying invention. And there were times, delicious times, when the outward conditions with which that imagination had to deal became transformed as by the wand of a magician. Days when the higher powers would be taken away from the house by outside duties, and the small domain would be untenanted save by the children. At such times, if the nursery rulers also happened to be propitious— on some holiday afternoon perhaps when it rained, and the schoolboys, the big brothers, found no amusement worthy of their attention out of doors —it would happen that the whole elder group would condescend to join us inferiors, would accommodate themselves to our fancies, talk for the nonce our jargon, play our plays, live in our world.

Then the house used to swell itself into a magical palace. A palace did I say?—a kingdom, a region. Every-day things dwindled and dwindled until we could not see them any more. The elders all combining with us to call that particular corner of the nursery a den of thieves, how unspeakably delicious it was! There must be thieves there if the others saw them too; it wasn't only Arthur's nonsense then, nor Annie's imagination. Thieves really did come, in some mysterious manner, through the wall, in the twilight of winter evenings. It was too delightful. Lucy herself saw a thief's eyes twinkle in the dusk, twice she felt a bony hand clutch at her from behind the window curtain; the children's hearts might well beat, their steps must fly indeed if they would reach a place of safety before the thieves could catch them.

And at last, when the place of safety had been
reached, and the elders perhaps suddenly decided
that all the thieves were dead, what did that matter?
the magic region need not fade away with them.
There was another story stranger and more en-
trancing far than the first, around which our thoughts
were always hanging, into which we were ready to
plunge at any moment and always with new delight.
A story, yes, a story that had no end, that seemed to
have grown up of itself and simply out of a name.
A dwarfed woman passed the house one rainy day
whilst two little faces were pressed against the
nursery window-pane, and four bright inquisitive
little eyes looked through, and, " That's Mrs. Calkill,"
said Arthur to Annie. That was all, but it was the
beginning of endless bliss. Who was Mrs. Calkill?
Annie knew, of course; she had known all about her
for ever so long, only somehow she had never thought
of mentioning her, but now she and Arthur had seen
her—they had both seen her by daylight in the street,
and they knew what her name was. It was Arthur
who knew her name, he must have known her too
then, they both knew her, there was a real Mrs.
Calkill. She was a fairy, very good, very clever, very
strict, very powerful. She could go about just as she
pleased anywhere, at any time; she knew what everybody was thinking about, and what all children did;
she governed her kingdom (the whole world) by
means of a system of rewards and of dreadful
punishments. She never allowed any one to see her
in her true fairy form; now and then she passed

down the street, on a wet day, under a green cotton umbrella almost as big as herself, but ordinarily she flew. She very seldom passed down the street, only once in a hundred years perhaps; certainly she never passed during the lifetime of the children after that one rainy day. So much the better, that showed that she was a fairy and not a woman; common people do the same thing over and over again, it is always something you least expect that happens about a fairy. Mrs. Calkill had a fairy palace, of course, somewhere, and we knew exactly what it was like, or, rather, we were in the course of knowing, for it would have taken a lifetime to sketch even the outlines of its endless, endless rooms; but *where* Mrs. Calkill's palace was, Annie herself did not know. Great was the delight of the little ones, then, when it was revealed to them upon one of those holiday afternoons that the second elder brother knew. It was miles and miles away, yet it was possible to get there and back within the hour of blind man's holiday; the road which led to it had scarcely ever been trodden by human foot, yet it opened from the inside of that very house in which the children were living; it led straight through their everyday world into the land of magic. If Mrs. Calkill should be very propitious, and should intimate as much, by a sign, to the brother with whom she had been secretly on terms of intimacy for a long time, he would take the children there himself, Annie describes one of these expeditions in her story of " Little Helen," in *Blind Man's Holiday.*

"If I were quite sure I could trust you," Cousin Stephen is made to say to little Helen, "I think I might perhaps introduce you to my friend Mrs. Calkill. She might not be very much vexed if I were to take you blindfold through the subterranean passage, and let you stand for five minutes in the enchanted palace garden." Then follows an account of the journey Helen takes—exactly like those which Annie remembered to have taken, blindfolded, in her childish days—up and down flights of stairs, and through rooms and passages of the house, whilst the little girl is made to believe that she is crossing streams, or scaling precipices, or walking through the caverns of Mrs. Calkill's underground kingdom.

After the enjoyment of such games as these; after racing for hours from hiding place to hiding place, after seeing, hearing, feeling, escaping from such dangers as those of the den of thieves; after the excitement of long blindfolded journeys to Magic Land, and of actual contact with the wonders there, grown-up people and nurses might talk as they pleased, might call things by commonplace names, might scold, and trouble, and fuss, but they could not rob us of our knowledge of the truth, they could not shut us up in the prison-house world from which we had had such escape, not for many many days to come at least.

But though we younger ones could thoroughly enter into these delights, and were ever ready to follow into the magical land, it was Annie who sowed the dream-seeds all about the home. I can fancy

that I see her now. The inspired child-face pondering at first, then smiling as at the suggestion of
joyous little spirits; then, as the fancies took shape
in her thoughts, the sweet eyes dilating with lights
and depths of mystery and fun, till at last the dear
lips opened that had always something so delightful
to say to us, with " Let us suppose now,"—and a new
world grew up around us, a world that might bloom
and fade indeed, but whose seed lay henceforth in its
outer self, a power of transformation latent after the
first breath of those magic words.

"This house is a story house," Annie makes
one of the children say in her tale of *Father Phim*,
when describing just such imaginative games as she
remembered to have played in her own childhood.
" All the rooms in it have got to be so many places
besides themselves, one never gets tired of them;
and the toys and the furniture have changed so
often, and done such curious things in our plays,
that when one looks at them, they seem to speak."

But it was not only in such a circumscribed sphere
that Annie's imagination busied itself; after the
house, the street, and, by and by, odd glimpses of
the town, flashed histories into the child's mind.

The town of Hull was not a very interesting
place as far as its natural features were concerned;
that part of it which Annie inhabited was composed
of a series of dull-looking streets of nearly unbroken uniformity. The country lay very far off;
the roads that led towards it were long and dreary,
scarcely any trees grew near them, and no flowers

bloomed on the strips of grass that bordered the pathways; level ground met the eye on every side: a hill, indeed, was a thing which it would have needed a strong imagination in any Hull child to picture to itself. Annie's walks when she was a child were chiefly taken along these roads, or up and down certain out-of-the-way streets near a waste bit of ground that had been prepared for building purposes, and afterwards deserted. This last place was her favourite resort, for it supplied a great deal of food to her imagination; there were rubbish-heaps and pits in it that served her for valleys and mountains, and which she loved to call by long-sounding names, taken hap-hazard from the pages of geography books.

Van Diemen's Land, one especially favoured part of this country was christened. It was bounded by a high wall of rough planks painted black, and Annie thought there must be something very wonderful behind those planks; if she could but see the other side of them she felt sure that some such discovery as that of Columbus would fall to her share. A story founded upon this reminiscence of her childhood forms one of the collection of tales spoken of before as published under the name of *Blind Man's Holiday*.

Sometimes it would be the interest in a single house that would absorb her, selected from its neighbours perhaps on account of some word that had been dropped about its inhabitants; or, again, it might be a passer-by, to whom one of the nursery group had chanced suddenly to give a name, as in the case of Mrs. Calkill, who would supply Annie with a story; the least thing was enough to give an impetus to her invention at any time. But whilst things, places, and grown-up people were as so many enchanted doors into the story world, children were much more than any of these to the child who was always longing to love as well as to know, and to whom the child-sphere outside the home was almost as full of tender interest as she afterwards described it to have been to her little heroine, Elsie, in her novel of *Oldbury*.

Annie's own first plunge into child-world, outside the family, was made in company with her own play-mate brother Arthur, when the two were sent to while away a few morning hours at a small, old-fashioned dame's school in the town. In one of the quietest streets of the quietest quarter there stood a row of narrow, three-storied houses, with flights of bright yellow stone steps leading up to the front doors—bright green doors that contrasted sharply with the yellow of the stones. How dull and silent all the houses seemed, how shut up they were—all excepting the house in which the two Miss Staintons lived, whose front door with its brass plate announcing an academy for young ladies and gentlemen, had to open so often to the knocks of the children, whose steps became sadly soiled by the dust of the little feet. To Annie the rooms of that school-house were more interesting than the palaces of Aladdin, or even than Mrs. Calkill's wonderful home. For in the

school there were children, real children, not
make-believe any more—acquaintances, companions,
friends. What a living wonder each one was to the
questioning new-comer, hungry to know what the
world was really like, or, rather, of what kind the
children were who inhabited it; whether their
experiences were like her own, whom they loved,
or how lovable they were.

Some of the children, too, had true histories
belonging to them, which they whispered to one
another across copy-books and slates and primers,
or at standstill places in sampler-working, whilst all
the energies of the good-natured Miss Stainton were
perhaps being brought to bear upon the dulness of
the child christened "Little Stupid" by her companions. Besides "Little Stupid," there was the
"sugar-plum child," who gave her sweets away, and
always had plenty of money to buy more. She was
rather spoilt at home, but had the most delightful
stories to tell about toys, and baby-houses, and
picture story-books in her nursery; there was the
thin, pale girl, who always moped, and never told
anybody anything about herself, so her history had
to be invented; there was the "prim little thing,"
who, by presence of mind, saved her grandmother
from being burnt—"Miss Miminy-Piminy," as Annie
christened her afterwards in *Blind Man's Holiday*.
The time and the place were brimful of tales.

Imperceptibly, the very childish things passed
away. In looking back it seems as if a new picture
had, unnoticed, been slidden across the view, and we

suddenly see an altered home, changed atmosphere, a different soil, fresh shoots beginning to be put forth by the small plant, another stage of life entered upon. The two elder brothers had grown up without our realising it, until at last they went, as it seemed, quite away—their visits to the home being paid at such long intervals that their lives ceased almost to touch the lives of the children. The other brothers, including Arthur, Annie's favourite playmate, went to a boarding-school in another county, and Annie only saw them at holiday times. The house became very quiet then. The eldest sister was occupied with teachers or friends, or paid long visits away from home; practically there were only three home children left—a baby brother, and Annie, and her youngest sister. At that time the two nearest in age began to draw close to one another; they felt somewhat as two shipwrecked sailors might have felt upon a desert island, and, indeed, they were almost as much alone. Besides the feeling of loneliness, they were conscious of a sensation of storms; the sky was not clear up above, as it had been used to be; troubles had swept by and had left cares behind. The heads of the parents began to be bowed by the passing of the years; their hearts were often heavy by reason of the burdens these brought them; they bore the burdens, and the children knew little of them, and understood less, but all the same they felt and reckoned the changes made by clouds as they passed overhead and cast shadows upon the ground.

Annie began to be delicate about this time, and had to be kept indoors during many weeks of the long cold springs which belong to the eastern coast. East wind and twilight are words which might be used to express the outward conditions of this stage of Annie's child-life. Yet there were compensations; if there was very little out-door life left for the children, and in the house, if there was but a silent nursery, a dull school-room, and many days, weeks even, dragged through in the weariness of childish illnesses, there was still the world of books to explore, enough in itself to compensate Annie for the absence of almost every other source of enjoyment. And besides the books, there was talk, interminable talk, between the sisters, who had now only each other to turn to for companionship, and who, as that companionship grew longer and closer, found a treasure in it which they never lost—the love that gladdened all their days. Reading and talking and love, these were the compensations of that time; it was then that the affectionateness, the true power of loving, began to be developed in Annie, for everything came from her first. Annie was the reader, Annie was the talker, Annie was the lover; her personality was the medium through which joy shone upon the life of the other. Annie was the reader—of children's books when she could get them. But children's books were scarce in those days; one can almost count them upon one's fingers. There were Mrs. Sherwood's *Fairchild Family*, her *Infant's Progress*, her *Henry and His Bearer*, her *Woodman and His*

Dog Cæsar. How the modern child would sneer at Mrs. Sherwood and her goody-goody tales! One sometimes wonders what the grown-up people of that generation would have thought of filling little heads with sensational stories of ragged London depravity, like those which do duty as Sunday books nowadays. But each age to its own liking. Mrs. Sherwood's homely inventions came quite naturally, and were very palatable food to the children of fifty years ago, and the remembrance of them is even beautiful in their eyes. Annie's imagination was greatly exercised at one time, I remember, by Mrs. Sherwood's story of the *Infant's Progress*, a childish version of the *Pilgrim's Progress* of Bunyan. The adventures in this tale turned chiefly upon the sayings and doings of a mysterious being, " Inbred Sin " by name, who was meant to be a personification of the inborn depravity of human nature. Why each child did not have a separate " Inbred Sin " to itself, it taxed her ingenuity to determine. In spite of this slight confusion of the allegory, however, the story pleased us so much that Annie turned it into a little play, which we acted amongst ourselves on Sunday afternoons in holiday times, when the brothers were at home and could help to supply the characters required by the piece. Then, Annie felt the great convenience of there being only one Inbred Sin for the whole group. Henry, the good boy of the party, always acted the tempter, and sometimes even, with blackened face, would personate the evil one himself, when that delightfully awful personage was

called upon to take a part in the performance. The
evil one supplemented Inbred Sin, it must be explained, in the story, opportunely popping in and
out to tempt and ruin the innocent little ones
whenever their natural tempter found himself
insufficient for the task.

Acting, however, could only be enjoyed in holiday times, talk filled the quieter seasons. Annie
took up the threads of the tales where the authors
laid them down, and continued the adventures
of the several characters, whose existences became
so real to us, that it seems, in looking back, as if
the lives of these persons had gone rippling on
side by side with ours through many many years.
It was with us at the time as though we were
surrounded by a troop of beings from whose sayings
and doings our attention could not distract itself, and
whose personalities exercised over ours a far stronger
influence than did any of those belonging to the
outward world, in which, at any rate, our bodies
lived and moved. The group we lived amongst was
a motley one, for the people who composed it had
gathered round us from times and places very wide
apart from one another. Annie's reading extended
to very different regions from any which the nursery
book-shelf could have led her to. The child made
raids, unknown to parents and teachers, upon the
down stairs library, where she filled her pockets
(very large loose pockets, tied on under the dress,
were worn in those days) with volumes of Rollin and
Plutarch, which she devoured afterwards in corners

of our own domain with silent delight. Rollin and
Plutarch were full of people, more real and more
interesting by far than any of Mrs. Sherwood's
creations. But how meagre the histories were after
all! How little they had to tell about Annie's
favourite characters! How many things must have
happened to Themistocles, for example, that nobody
had ever thought of writing down. Themistocles
was Annie's pet hero. "Strike, but hear me," was
only the greatness of him gathered up into a nut-
shell; in his life there had doubtless been numberless crises, in which his magnanimity had been just
as strikingly displayed.

How well I can recall the winter twilight in
our low square room, the toys and books all
thrown aside for the moment, heaped up in corners,
a clear space in the middle of the floor, the red
fire-glow, the weird shadows upon the walls cast
by oil-lamps in the street outside, the kettle upon
the hob—not even having begun its singing—a
happy pervading consciousness that the tea-hour
had not nearly come, and that a long stretch of time
to ourselves lay before us. And then the walk round
and round the room amongst the changing lights and
shades in such companionship, holding such converse.
Socrates was there, he walked with us, and talked,
not with us, certainly, but intimately, in our hearing,
with his noble and beautiful friends; Alcibiades was
there, and Plato and Pericles, and Themistocles was
there also—he and Socrates met for the first time
in our playroom—and they were friends. Socrates

could find no fault, no ignorance, in the great Athenian.

P. D., standing for "pleasant discourse," not for " Platonic Dialogues," was the name Annie gave to this sort of story conversation, and we never tired of it. It came to be almost as necessary as daily bread to us, and Annie was rarely behindhand with the supply. She was in truth instant in season and out of season, for the talks were not restricted to twilight hours or to playtimes in general. We were left very much alone to prepare lessons for our teachers, or to practise jingling duets upon a jingling piano, and whenever trusted in this manner, we proved ourselves singularly unworthy of the confidence. It was always the same thing as far as I can remember; half a sum worked out, a couple of bars of music played, and then a long rest for slates and pencils, and copy-books and piano. A sudden end reached of all that sort of thing, and the door thrown wide open into the land we loved, and then our troop of friends came through and chatted delightfully with us until the opening of some strangely actual wooden door ·close upon us revealed to our startled gaze the daily governess perhaps, or the frumpy old music-mistress, bewigged and snuffy, for all the world like ghosts from some uncomfortable icy region invading our gay company, as uncongenial to it as any poor plague-stricken mortal could have been to the ladies and gentlemen of the *Decamerone*. Of course we were scolded, but that did not make any lasting impression; scolding and discomfort belonged naturally to the outside world, and the only lesson to be learned from them was that we should conduct our dishonesty more discreetly another time —keep our ears open to knocks at the front door in fact, so as to be able to assume the requisite appearance of industry in the nick of time.

It would seem that Annie had not much con- scientiousness at this period of her existence, and yet there was a soft spot in her conscience, and through all these careless hours, a chamber of reason in her brain which she was prompted to enter now and then, and where she counted up the sum of gain or loss. Sometimes it would be the recollection of a story that led her there, or it might be the haunting words of some text that a preacher had used as the refrain of his discourse ; such, for example, as, " Pray ye that your flight be not in the winter," or, " The harvest is passed, the summer is ended, and ye are not saved." Texts of this kind seemed to have a sort of fitful fascination for Annie, who was subject all her life to acute attacks of regret and remorse. I think that the words about summer and the harvest first touched her with a sense of seriousness and sadness in the passing of time. There was also a little story that she must have first read when quite a child, which made a strong and lasting im- pression upon her mind. It was called *The Warning Clock*, and told in a sort of allegory the tale of a wasted life. There was a picture at the beginning of the book of a little girl lying comfortably asleep in bed. A clock hung against the wall of the room

in which she was, with its hands pointing to the hour
of morning, an old nurse was just drawing aside the
bed-curtain, trying to rouse the young sleeper. The
child is made to wake up and say, " Call me again,
nurse, in an hour's time, then I will get up." That
was the history of her day, " Call me again in
an hour's time." And every hour the nurse came,
and stood at the foot of the bed, and called the child
by her name, and each hour the clock struck a fresh
note of warning, until at last the hour of midnight
came. There was the picture of the dark room, the
clock with its warning fingers fixed at twelve, no
kind nurse at the bedside, but instead, in the doorway, the figure of a man whose face was veiled, and
who held a lantern in his hand, the day's last messenger, of whom the story affirmed that " he would
brook no delay." The child sat up in bed, wringing
her hands with a look of agony upon the little face.
There was a weird suggestion of horror through it
all. The day was over, the night had come, and a
life was lost.

When Annie fell into a fit of seriousness in her
young days, dreaming was the sin of which her conscience invariably accused her—of dreaming away her
life instead of living it. "The spring is passing, the
summer is coming, the harvest will soon be here,"
the words and the images hurried through her mind,
and then with a sudden compelling wish to see something clearly, to clutch hold of some reality, she
would push aside all the dear fantasies, and break
through the shadow world.

She announced her stern resolve to me. " I have
been thinking it all over," she would say, "we are
wasting our time, we are dreaming away our lives.
We won't do it any more. Let us give up our foolish
talking and dreaming, and begin at once to be in
earnest: let us be in earnest in improving ourselves,
and let us begin with our thoughts." Then she
would expound one of the papers in a collection of
tales and essays by Jane Taylor, on the government
of the thoughts, and invite me to set my face with
hers steadily towards better things. Of course I
tried to follow where my magician led, but, oh dear !
it was like a dripping, rainy day, as we stumbled
side by side along the dreary road of self-improve-
ment, with the corpses of our dead delights lying
stark on either side. The resolution never lasted for
many days together, however, the dead images soon
springing up again into life. This habit of living in
the world of invention became at certain times so
mixed up with the outward life as to produce what I
may almost call events in our childhood. One such
period stands out from the rest.

Annie had got hold of a book written by Mrs.
Sherwood called *The Nun*, a tale of convent life, the
scene of which was laid somewhere in France; the
two principal heroines, Pauline and Clarice, became
by some means converted to the Protestant faith, and
the plot of the book consisted in the history of the
persecutions they endured at the hands of the bigoted
Mother Superior and the sisters, their subsequent
adventures, and final escape from thraldom.   The

plot was rather a clever one, and the details were graphically given ; it was as absorbing to us as any sensational novel could have been. The part of the tale that attracted us most was that relating to one of the side characters, a very old nun, " la mère Agnes," who, on account of her obstinate denial of certain tenets of the Catholic faith, had, when quite young, been hidden away in a cell underground, that she might not contaminate the sisterhood. In this concealment she had grown old, her health had been broken, her intellect enfeebled. She lay upon a heap of straw in a corner of her cell, and had never seen or spoken to a human being since she had entered her living tomb, the daily pittance of bread and water being thrust in to her through a hole in the dungeon's wall. It was so long since " la mère Agnes " had been buried that her very existence was unknown to the younger members of the community, until Pauline or Clarice discovered the fearful secret, and then it was passed on from sister to sister in awe-struck whispers from behind their veils. There was just the sort of chill about this part of the story calculated to enhance enjoyment of the sunshiny end of the book, where Pauline and Clarice, each meeting with a gallant young Protestant deliverer, married comfortably, and remained in safety and happiness the rest of their days.

That any human being could be hidden away in a house, and so securely hidden that, though the house were full of people, the majority of them should know nothing at all about it, might never

even have heard of the concealed person, was a new,
delightful, bewildering idea. Who could say where
such a hidden one might not be ? A nun might be
imprisoned in any house. There were several
Roman Catholics in the town, and very bigoted
ones, we knew. Father Render, the head of them,
had held a controversy once with our own father—in
which, of course, he had been worsted. What more
likely than that he should, ever since his defeat,
have been burning to revenge himself upon somebody.
He would not go to work openly—no Roman Catholic
ever did ; he would wreak his vengeance upon some
weak undefended creature; in short, he would take
a nun, and shut her up in a cell or dungeon somewhere. He would not be particular as to the where-
abouts he should select, so long as he could find a
dungeon to his mind; and now that we came to
think of it, what was there above the trap-door in
the housemaid's cupboard ? Where did it lead to ?
Nowhere, as far as we could see. And what could it
be that lay underneath the long passage between the
cupboard and the spare bed-room ? Nobody could
make this clear to us. Those we asked either could
not, or would not, or dared not, say ; we decided that
they could not, and with the sudden thrill of a new,
enchanting hope, settled it that we could. A subterranean gallery lay under the one; a prison in the roof
was above the other. Father Render's nun, poor
thing, was shifted to and fro between these ; sometimes she dwelt in the cold, and sometimes she was
shut up in the darkness.

The story, as Annie invented it, hung very well
together; it sounded more than possible, it seemed
likely. We talked about it and thought about it, and
hoped that it was true, until, at last, we really felt as
if it were so, and, oddly enough, we acted as we felt.
We saved up our cakes and biscuits and other little
luxuries for the prisoner, fastening packets of these
to the handle of a long broom, and poking them
through a crevice in the trap-door, whilst we believed,
or tried to believe, that she could receive them. We
wrote notes to the nun assuring her of our sympathy
and of our determination to set her free; and these
also we sent up by means of the friendly broom. We
looked, oh ! how longingly, for her replies. We remembered that she had no paper to write upon, so
we sent up blank sheets and a pencil. After that we
did find a scrap of writing-paper one day, very much
crumpled, and dirtied with coal-dust, in the housemaid's hearth box ; there was no writing upon it, but
perhaps it was intended for a sign. We tried hard
not to be discouraged, though our friend's reticence
was difficult to explain ; she had grown to be suspicious through ill-treatment, Annie thought, and who
could wonder ? Yet she might begin to relax a little
towards such red-hot Protestants as ourselves. More
likely it was fear which withheld her from giving the
desired sign—mortal dread of her deadly enemy, that
bloodthirsty Father Render.

In our walks about the town we passed the good
priest sometimes, frocked and shaven, but of a burly,
good-natured, rubicund presence withal, and we only

thought the worse of him on account of his innocent
looks. I almost think that we formed vigorous reso-
lutions of standing firmly in front of his path, and
denouncing before all passers by the foulness of his
secret deeds ; but we contented ourselves with scowls
and whispers when the meeting-times really came,
and with a shuddering recoil from the contamination
of contact with such a black-hearted son of Belial.
Yet we might well have been grateful to him for
lending his personality to the construction of a story
which was certainly the source of a good deal of
happiness to us for a long time. How hard-hearted
children are ! I don't think there was anything we
dreaded much more than the discovery that our
little tragedy had no existence in fact, that there
was no nun after all wearing away her miserable
days on the very borders of our careless life.

At last Annie determined that the time had
come when we must strike a decided blow for the
deliverance of the prisoner. She had given up the
theory of the roof-prison just then, and was convinced
that the subterranean gallery concealed our unfortunate friend. We began to consider the possibility of
taking up one of the planks of the floor, and as we
were not strong enough to accomplish this feat alone
we determined to take one or two friends into our
confidence. We had not many child companions, but
there were two families—the grand-daughters of a
certain highly-respected clergyman, a patriarch among
the pastors of the town—with whom we were allowed
to be intimate, and whom we met on birthdays and

half-holidays, and such-like festive occasions. Just at
the time when the nun mania was at its height, and
when we had resolved to divulge our secret, it chanced
that one of these meetings took place. Five or
six little girls assembled in our play-room for tea
and talk. After tea the talk began; Annie gathered
the children round her, told her story, and opened
out her plans. She made our friends understand
that she had selected them to be partners with us in
a great and glorious undertaking to be carried out
that very evening,—the breaking of the prison-
doors and letting the prisoner go free. Strange to
say, our friends were at first hard to convince that
what Annie told them was actually true, and stranger
still, when convinced, they were far from being
pleased with the idea. Some said they did not like
to hear about the nun or Father Render; one or two
cried, and all of them declared that the story
frightened them very much indeed. Annie, however,
was not to be daunted; she asserted, she argued, she
convinced.

By the time the sceptics had been talked into
something like the submission of their private
judgment, and had agreed to assist in the great act
of the drama, twilight had given place to darkness,
and a chill, eerie feeling was creeping over us all.
There was one sweet little girl in the group, Fanny
by name, who had been amongst the first to take
the matter seriously, and yet had not given way to
childish fears; she soothed and strengthened her
sisters and cousins; she looked so sweet, and wise, and

reliable, that the halters began to look up to her as a sort of leader, and when the darkness drew us all into a closer fellowship, she made us kneel down while she offered up a prayer for the success of our undertaking. After this, with lighted candle, with chisel and hammer, we all, Annie and Fanny leading the way, proceeded to the scene of danger.

The staircase and the passage and the empty room beyond looked unusually dark that evening, the atmosphere of them felt unaccountably chilly, an awful stillness reigned. At last Annie broke the stillness by dealing a few vigorous blows with her hammer upon the floor, and then, some shrieking, some weeping, all struck with mortal terror, the whole party turned and fled—all the followers at least —amongst whom there was a general *sauve qui peut* until the play-room had been regained, and our ears were safe from the sounds of those awful echoes that had assailed them from the prison underground.

Meanwhile Annie and Fanny, scorning to fly with the *canaille*, remained behind the rest long enough to assure themselves that no further action could be effected at that time, and then, disappointed and crestfallen, they joined us below. The occasion had come and gone then, and all remained as before ! Alas ! no—not all. Nothing could restore the equanimity of our young companions ; sobs and hysterics wound up the little *fête*. Finally, the nursemaids came, and our friends could not conceal the delight they felt in quitting our company. Everybody went away; we looked at each other, and felt very flat indeed. We did not talk much about the nun the next morning, being anxious to persuade ourselves that there had not been any real crisis in her affairs, nor any collapse, but somehow it would not do; our inner world had been shaken, and the outer world would not let us alone. Notes flew about the whole of the following day between the parents of the two families of cousins and our parents; a messenger even called from one of the houses to expostulate concerning the kind of amusement that had been provided for the little guests; one of them had not been able to sleep the whole night, another was almost raving about a nun, and a dungeon, and the priest. Could any clue be found by which to unravel such strange confusion,—was there any foundation in fact for the scandal, or was the whole story a purposeless, mischief-making invention concocted in the clergyman's household?

Put in this way, our romance did not seem interesting any longer; it assumed an ugly appearance, and we began to feel somewhat ashamed of it. Arthur, too, happened to come home about that time, and we could see that he was incredulous—worse than incredulous; he counted the whole affair to have been a very silly piece of business indeed. So died our nun, and the clouds of our delusion rose and spread away, and melted into thinnest vapour, and we were left below, unclothed, as it were, for some short space, of any enshrouding dream.

Arthur's presence during his holidays was generally unfavourable to dreams, or, rather, he brought in such a different set of ideas, and told so many marvellous histories from his experience of real school-life, that he was apt to draw Annie out of her world into one of his making. It was a great change from thinking about the nun, or from following out any of our other story talk, to listen to all the curious quirks and sayings of the drill-sergeant at his school, whom Arthur mimicked to us, or to contemplate a picture of the French master's despair when the entire class deserted his teaching for the pursuit of rats and mice. In short, our lives were periodically sharpened and brightened by the fun which we shared with our brothers during their home-comings. The youngest brother, too, was growing up into a playfellow, and fits of companionship with him made many gaps in our dream world.

Occasionally the boys shared—I was going to say our instruction, but it would be more correct to say our instructors, for we were all of us dead against being taught. Passive resistance to the encroachments which masters or mistresses made upon our time we were always ready to offer; the boys invented more active measures. We tired our two French masters with our idle fun ; but it was with the unfortunate man supposed to teach us writing and arithmetic that we chiefly exercised ourselves. Sometimes through a long course of this master's visits we amused ourselves by serving up for our lesson one particular question in the Rule of Three, with slightly varying adjuncts, but never so carefully disguised as to impose upon a second glance ; and when the bewildered

teacher came out with his habitual remonstrance (in
strong Yorkshire accent), "By the by, miss, I conceive you've brought me fifty coos again ; the fact is,
you astonish me, miss ; it pricks me to the 'art, miss
—it does indeed," we received the announcement
with unfailing delight, and with expressions of
innocent surprise in the discovery that we had ever
come across such a question as that touching the
fifty cows before.

The town we lived in had many salient points
and salient characters belonging to it, which Arthur
had the happy knack of bringing into prominence.
Arthur and Annie studied the manners and the
people of Hull together. The original of the Miss
Berry of *Oldbury* lived in Hull, as full of charming
simplicity and delightful little oddities and kind
affectionate ways as her shadow sister remains now.
The real Miss Berry had her great map of Scripture events and characters such as Annie described
afterwards.

The holding of religious meetings was one of the
most important features of life, in our town. There
was every possible variety of societies in whose
behalf these assemblies were held, but the chief
amongst them all was the Church Missionary Society.
The whole religious world of Hull combined to do
honour to the yearly meetings of that society, held
inside the largest church of the place. The towns-
people flocked in families to the church on those
occasions, when instead of the pulpit a large platform covered with green baize faced the congregation ;

chairs were studded over the platform, and in the
middle there stood a table with glasses of water upon
it, and a dish of delicious-looking oranges, wherewith
the clergymen were wont to refresh themselves when
wearied with their discourses. To the eyes of us
children, that old green baize platform was just a
symbol of the comfortable side of religion, saying to
us once every year, "Now we are going to have a
right pleasant time of it together," and we did have
decidedly amusing times, listening to queer stories
about the heathen, regaling ourselves with sweet
biscuits, of which all children were allowed a liberal
supply at meetings, putting money into the plate
at the collection, and finally going home rather late
in the afternoon with a consciousness of having
had a jolly holiday, and of having, at the same
time, advanced the world a stage or two towards
the millennium.

Next in importance to the religious meeting, in
children's eyes, stood the Friday party—occasions on
which the clergymen met at one another's houses for
Bible reading and discussion. Certainly these good
priests did not fast on Fridays, at any rate not at
tea; the Bible discussions were always inaugurated
by a meal, one of those real Yorkshire teas of which
a south country person can have no idea, when piles
and piles of hot buttered cakes are served up and
made away with. We children used to hang about
the retreating trays as the waiters came in and out,
for the double purpose of picking up a scrambling
repast, and of catching some tones from the hubbub

of talk going on inside the drawing-room. Finally,
when the doors were closed, and the elders occupied
themselves with the serious part of the business, we
four took refuge in the empty portions of the house,
dressed up in the clergymen's hats and coats, and
held a mimic missionary meeting all to ourselves. It
was a happy day for us when we discovered that we
could amongst us reproduce almost exactly the tones
and manners of the several ministers, which we
generally did in the words of the favourite missionary hymn, "O'er the realm of pagan darkness," a
verse for each clergyman in turn all round.

Hull was distinctly a party place. The town was
capable of dividing itself upon any question almost
—as to whether rice is grown upon mud or water,
for example; indeed, there was a tradition that a
section of it did once actually fall into a position of
antagonism on that debatable ground. But it would
generally be some question of politics that set the
little world on fire. Conservative or Radical, that
was the question of questions; blue or yellow, as the
distinction displayed itself before our eyes, the rival
colours becoming signs of great living realities. Blue
—that meant, naturally, high breeding, good looks,
courage, generosity, faithfulness to country and to
God. Yellow—that signified, deformity, degradation,
drunkenness, injustice, baseness of all kinds, fighting
and Atheism. Even a golden lily used to look quite
wicked beside a blue fleur de lys.

One election stands out among the rest as having
particularly excited the town, especially the ladies of

it, not on account of any especial question of politics
involved in it, but because of unusual interest that
attached to the persons of the candidates on that occasion. One was a Wilberforce, the other was a young
baronet—touchingly young, the ladies pronounced
him to be, and about him spinster imagination unceasingly busied itself. He was known to be a scion
of the aristocracy too, and that was a fact particularly
commendable in Hull eyes; whilst there was something plebeian in the very names of the rival candidates, Clay and Hutt. The general enthusiasm was
catching, and "Don't you think," Annie said, one day,
"that there must be something very remarkable in
the new member?" The time just then happened
to be favourable for inventions; there had been
a theme missing in Annie's story-talk for some
time, ever since the collapse of the nun romance, in
fact, and she readily seized upon an idea for a new
tale. The member became the hero of many
volumes of her unpublished novels, and connected with these there grew up one of the strangest
fancies, I think, that Annie ever originated. "Let
us imagine," she said, "that there is a man called a
Writer, who can see into every house just as he
pleases, and who writes down all that he sees in
stories called 'scenes' that he gives us to read."
"Yes—well—let us imagine it," and we did, until
the Writer became an ever-present idea in our
minds. He was an omnipresent kind of being
almost, for while he was supposed to go about to
distant places and bring back scenes to Annie, his

partner in novel-writing, he was still always looking
through one particular corner of the ceiling, in
whatever room we happened to be, an observer
and recorder from whom we could never escape.
Occasionally when there was any remark we wished
to make about any one, which we did not wish to
be generally known, we used to feel ourselves
obliged to write it down upon slates or paper, and
pass the writing to and fro. Still we never felt the
Writer a *gêne;* he had become so necessary to the
"scenes" we delighted in that we willingly put up
with any trifling annoyance he might cause us in our
everyday life. Long after we had ceased to talk
story-talk of any kind, the impression of that
mysterious personage, the Writer, sitting always overhead and looking through the roof of one's house,
remained as a sort of slumbering belief in our minds.

Annie's inventions and dreaming were always
entirely impersonal; she never by any chance, I
think, built a castle in the air about herself or her
own future, as many young people are in the habit
of doing; all thoughts of self were crowded out by
an absorbing realisation of her own creations. It
was with her, she used to say, as if she were watching
the progress of one interminable tale, in which her
own being bore no part, and over which her own will
exercised no control; she just stood apart, and
watched perpetually, like some Lady of Shalott, the
passing and repassing of sweet shades, listening to
their converse, waiting upon their actions, grieving
at their sorrows, rejoicing in their joy.

One or two circumstances combined to make outside life more interesting to Annie as years passed on, and foremost among these was her being taught for the first time by a teacher whom she could really love.

The new governess, a young girl, had the happy knack of making duty seem a pleasant thing; she and Annie drew together at once, and an easy kind of sisterly relationship established itself between them. Annie Norman was original in her methods of instruction; sometimes she would throw away all books and give up entire days to talk, and Annie certainly learned much more from these opportunities of free intercourse with an original mind than she would have done through a system of unbroken routine. The young teacher had a remarkable power of reading character, and as Annie had a similar gift, it was both delightful and helpful to her to exchange her own crude thoughts with the equally fresh but more exercised deductions of her companion.

When quite a child Annie had been fond of expounding her views upon character; one long Sunday evening's talk on such subjects I especially remember, when we recorded the event in a little pocket diary: "Had a real talk about real things."

Annie worked out in her own mind on that occasion that all persons in the world must belong to one of four classes: North, South, East, or West.

North—hard, cold, reasonable people.

South—impulsive, imaginative, sympathetic.

East—negative and stupid.

West—sentimental and unreal.

The idea was a rough attempt at the classification of people according to temperament, not very unlike the theory of Jacob Boehme, set forth in his *Treatise of the Four Temperaments*, in which he speaks of Earth, Air, Fire, and Water natures. Annie came upon Jacob Boehme's book in later years and took great pleasure in it.

At last the shock of a great fear broke upon the family, scattering for the time all Annie's absorbing fancies, and clouding over the pleasure of her new-found friendship. The suffering of the father had been increasing year by year, until a crisis came, and the word was spoken that death might be near. Then there came a time in which nothing can be distinguished through the mist of tears and tumultuous fears and hopes, regrets and passionate blind prayers. In all this there was a greater shock for Annie than for any of the other younger ones, because she, amongst them, loved the father most; besides, there was the horror of a dark reality having struck into the midst of her ideal world.

The fear passed away, and the father's life was given back, sunk deeper into suffering and weakness, both of which were borne with such unfailing patience that it was only too easy for children to forget them. I doubt whether even Annie fretted much at that time about any of his added pain; still the anxiety of the crisis closed an era in her inner life. She passed on after that to a more pressing sense of responsibility, and of the contrast between living and dreaming: remorse for the one more frequently than before interfered with the happiness of the other.

One result of the father's illness was the removal of the home party for an entire summer to his country rectory. Annie had seen very little of real country life so far, nothing more than could be obtained during the yearly visit to a tiny watering-place at the mouth of the Humber, whose principal features were·a low, flat, sandy common, and a rather muddy expanse of waters. Spite of all deficiencies of the place, however, Annie's life-long pleasure in the sea and in all sea sights and sounds was born of her sojourns there, with the family gatherings, holiday excursions, and bright, windy days upon the shore. But Cleathorpes was not to be compared with Nunnington, the picturesque village at the foot of the Yorkshire moors, where one long perfect summer of Annie's life was passed.

Annie afterwards laid the plot of her first published children's tale, *Mia and Charlie*, at Nunnington, and in it she happily describes some of the scenery and characteristics of the place. It must have been a great pleasure to her, one thinks, to find in the tumble-down, old-fashioned rectory, a realisation of some of her early fancies, a house that really had strange nooks in it, and unused shadowed rooms. From the windows of some of the rooms one could walk out on to the side of a hill that was a garden too, from whose sloping green terraces the village down below was visible, with its bright little river running through ;

and far away the lines of softly curving hills
against the sky. It was there that nature first spoke
to Annie, with the double voice she ever afterwards
loved so well, listening for and trying to understand
the suggestion, the emotion, the thought of every
pictured word.

The life she lived at Nunnington was a
thoroughly healthy one—real family life such as had
not been enjoyed by her for years. In the quiet of
the little place, removed as all were from companionship outside the home circle, and during the leisure
of long summer days, it was easy for all differences
of age and diversities of taste to meet and mingle.
To the mother that season was like an epoch out of
the beloved past lived over again, and her whole
nature rejoiced in it; the father had come to his
country rectory to seek health and rest, and though
reading was his one idea of healthy enjoyment, he
would sometimes pass an hour or two with his
children in outdoor sunshine, and at any rate there
was always an atmosphere of joy wherever he and
his books were found together. During his holiday,
too, there was leisure for hunting out fresh books for
Annie to carry away to her favourite unused garret,
where she feasted upon them for hours together. In
her walks through the country lanes, whose summer
roses and whose autumn hips and haws were glorious
treasures to town-bred children, Annie began the
study of botany, to which she frequently returned
with pleasure at other periods of her life. It was
one of the few amusements besides reading that

helped to soothe the pain-stricken days of her last
summer upon earth, when she eagerly welcomed any
little newly-found flower, or insignificant weed even,
which friends brought to her from distances she was
no longer able to reach. As well as botany, natural
history began to claim her attention, and she gave
many hours in her garret to the study of a book on
insect life by Kirby and Spence, the facts of which
were laid up with other heterogeneous matter in the
treasure house of her memory, and drawn upon for
the construction of many of her children's stories,
notably *Little Wanderlin,* where the characters and
ways of birds, and beasts, and fish, wind in and out
amongst the more strictly fairy-like inventions with
a pleasant interchange of fact and fable.

The eldest sister began to draw Annie up into
companionship with her about this time, from which
dated the true heart and mind friendship that ever
afterwards existed between the two, gifted with
almost equally strong social instincts and quick perceptions of character. Annie interested herself in
studying the people of Nunnington. There were
farmers' families in the neighbourhood, of a pleasant
old-fashioned Yorkshire type—rudely healthy, shrewd,
yet superstitious, for a firm belief in witchcraft still
obtained amongst them : hard-working people, father,
mother, sister, and brother, sharing outdoor occu-
pation, sharing also, sister with brother, the same
uncouth ways, the same unsensitive temperaments.
Some of the groups formed really beautiful subjects
for study : the hale old people ; the strong well-built

men; the girls, not so much modest, as more than
usually free from self-consciousness—all excepting the
beauties amongst them, that is to say, who would be
apt to find rake or hay fork irksome, and to look
askance during careless handling of the same, with
a pretty assurance in their smiling eyes that good
looks were a better dowry than helpfulness or riches
would ever prove. Of all the houses Annie visited
none attracted her imagination more than did Nunnington Hall itself, an old Manor House, deserted for
the time by its owners, which had a tale belonging
to it, and about whose shady avenues, and through
whose empty, tapestried rooms Annie loved to
wander and dream. The story told about the Hall
had a stepmother in it, and a sickly child, and some
horrible catastrophe, with a suspicion of murder
lurking round it, and a ghost—a lady in silk, who
came and went with awful faint rustle up and down
the broad oak staircase, and looked with pale face
from an upper turreted window upon the silent
sward below. Annie introduced her into *Mia and
Charlie*, where she slightly sketched the legend.
She had a half-formed intention of working up the
details some day into a full-grown romance; that
purpose, however, she never fulfilled, but she had the
pleasure of seeing the story receive shape and beauty
at her suggestion, by the hand of a sister novelist
in the pages of *Doris Barugh*.

Another trifling incident connected with this
country summer may be worth mentioning, as having
perhaps had some slight influence on Annie's

thoughts and character. She paid her first visit from home, in company with her eldest sister, at the house of some grown-up young cousins, to whom she came as one of their own standing, and no longer as a child. The atmosphere of the home was unlike anything Annie had ever experienced before. Our own family life had always been ordered very soberly, almost puritanically, with its strictly kept Sunday, quaker-like plainness of costume, and emptiness of all amusement. That of our young relatives was set up upon a very different model. The girls, just eagerly entering into life, had never been enjoined to renounce the world; it could never have struck them that to dress prettily and becomingly was otherwise than wise and right; the pleasures of society were natural, healthful pleasures to them; ball-going did not seem less innocent to them than a scamper on horseback across country, or a summer ramble in the fields, and certainly no pleasures they had indulged in had spoiled their really unworldly natures, or deadened the fresh warm-heartedness which made them always ready to share their good things with others, admiration amongst the rest. Mrs. Sherwood's ball-going young lady had always been depicted as selfish, hard-hearted, reckless, with ruin for her portion in this world, and damnation as her retribution in the next; but these generous girls, sunned by prosperity, seemed to be far enough from the first, and nowhere within sight of the second. The contradiction may well have puzzled Annie, and perhaps helped to awake in her the fairness with.

which she was given to estimate the prejudices of others. Annie fell much in love with her cousins, and all, it need scarcely be said, fell much in love with her; it was they who first told her that she was beautiful, and I am sure that the knowledge was good for her. Although Annie was exceptionally sweet-looking, her parents had always spoken to her of her appearance as if she were unfortunately plain. It was the habit of religious people in those days to throw such dishonour upon the flesh, and the next best thing to not having good looks was held to be not knowing that you had them. Thus the parents had striven to shield the pretty one as long as possible from the evil of her fate, but one little word, one admiring look, tore the veil away.

Annie was about fifteen at the time of which we are speaking—her beauty of a tall, fair, and aquiline type which she had inherited from her father with her Irish blood. Her colouring was rich, her hair light brown with a golden hue in it. Her eyes were very beautiful, large and blue, expressing every change of thought and feeling, her broad forehead giving at the same time a certain steadiness and sense of power. From her childhood she had been a little deaf, and this infirmity combined with her natural disposition to give to her face and figure an air partly pensive and partly deferential. In Annie's case the effort to mislead her about her looks had been ill-judged. She was naturally as far as possible from being self-occupied, but it depressed her and went far towards crushing her upon self-regardful thoughts, to be told that she was personally incapable of pleasing. The discovery that, after all, this was an exaggeration or a mistake must have marked a stage in her inner life, and may have felt something like the laying aside of fettering garments, and moving pleasurably in clothes that fit and are becoming. Here we may say that childhood ends, here girlhood first guesses at its charm; we leave the bud to search into the sweetness of the flower; here the beautiful summer came to its end also, and the leisure and the pause in the lives young and old that had sheltered together in its sunshine and its rest.

PART II.

BOARDING-SCHOOL life was Annie's next experience. With school, the ideal school, her child imagination had been familiar; tales of school life having taken their turn amongst scenes, P. D., and other story conversation, when teachers and scholars, companionship and talk were mapped out with great clearness, set in a charming haze of indefinable possibilities. School real was, perhaps, not much like school ideal, but the time that Annie spent there was made rich by the forming of one or two friendships as beautiful as any which her imagination had drawn. Amongst the girls Annie soon became a great favourite; with the teachers, and with the modes of instruction which obtained at the school, she was not so much in accord.

The week-day classes ran a curious dull little round. English, Grecian, and Roman histories were read by turns, half an hour being allowed for each at a time ; the pupils looked at the backs of the books, to be quite sure where they were.

Annie was never thought exactly clever by her instructors ; out-of-the-way scraps of knowledge came

so much more readily to hand with her than did just
the particular things that she was expected to have
at her fingers' ends, and a thirst for any sort of knowledge outside the ordinary school routine was not a
distinguishing feature of the place.

"Lizzie, of what were you and Annie Keary talking so eagerly in the garden during the English
speaking hour?" was asked on one occasion by the
head teacher in the school.

Confusedly, yet with a slight impression of new
and growing importance, the reply came from Lizzie,
"Oh, madame! Annie Keary was telling me all
about gravitation and the stars."

Very long faces all round, and "H'm, it's a pity,
I think, that Miss Keary cannot find something
more edifying to say to her companions, since she
appears to be so fond of talking," was the freezing
rejoinder.

There was one subject, the subject of religion,
which the head of the school was never weary of
bringing before her pupils, and it was the only one
that possessed any real importance in her eyes. Her
influence over many of the girls, religiously, was
very great; to the one mind with which I am dealing I do not think that her teachings on this subject
were helpful. Our teacher thought clearly, and
expressed herself with great force. She spoke to
her household twice every day, at morning and at
evening prayers; sometimes she would talk very
beautifully of the love of God, and then, holding
the shut Bible between her hands, would . wind

up her discourse in some such terms as the following :—

" Here," she would say, " between these boards is shut up Eternal Life, and to-day it is offered to each one of you ; take it to-day, to-morrow it may be too late. For if the Spirit should cease to strive with you, though you may call, He will not hear. Not one of you who has heard the message here can find excuse in the day of judgment. If you are lost, you will see the name of this very house where I have spoken to you written upon the floor of hell— your opportunity turned into your condemnation."

Some of the girls were brought to think seriously by her means; some were hardened. Annie tried simply to put the subject away from her, and so her spiritual growth was arrested at this time. I say arrested, because her spirit had felt some upward motion of life during that summer when she had come out from her dreams in the genial home, had begun to look at nature with loving, understanding eyes, and had first become conscious of the dim longings and sweet emotions of youth.

The teaching of Mr. Baker, the pastor of the school, who, conducted the Church services every Sunday in the great school-room, were of a less exciting nature than were those of the mistress. Sundays gave the girls something of rest spiritually, not mentally by any means. Mr. Baker's sermon was the absorbing topic of the day. All the lady teachers took notes of the morning discourse, and at noon gathered the pupils around them to superintend their writing out of the sermon from memory.

"Miss White," one teacher would sometimes ask of another, "can you help me to the ninth small head under dear Mr. Baker's fifth large head to-day?"

Annie, who on account of her deafness found it very difficult to follow the words of the preacher, was apt to draw largely upon her imagination in the writing out of the sermon; and her class teacher used to wax very wroth with her on that account.

"Annie Keary," she exclaimed one Monday morning, as she was settling herself to the task of reading over a pile of sermon copy-books, "Annie Keary, what do you think I am doing now? Praying for patience before I read *your* version of dear Mr. Baker's precious words! Do you know that you put your own feeble expressions instead of his? Listen to this (opening the book at a venture and reading a paragraph) those are *your* words, Miss Keary, put instead of the very cream of the discourse. Take the book away, and let me have something to read that I can understand."

Or it might be a pathetic appeal to the neighbouring teacher at her table seated before a similar pile of books.

"My dear Miss Green, what do you think Miss Keary has written down here?"

"Oh! my dear Miss Ewin, don't ask me; I've quite ceased to be surprised at anything which Miss Keary may say or write."

The pleasant companionship she had, and the many friendships she formed, made up to Annie for any other shortcomings of school life. I can see her the centre of one of the groups. There was tall handsome Marion, the original of Rosamond in *Janet's Home ;* there was Catherine, with the large melting eyes, brimful of self-consciousness, that were so subtle, so changeful in their charm. Catherine's was the only talk that used to ripple over into that forbidden land where lovers obtruded themselves, whose looks and sayings were so enigmatical that they had to be discussed and explained—a perfectly new region this to Annie, who had no personal experience of such matters, and was proportionally interested in the talk of a young girl who had begun to sip the real cup of life. Then there was Cecil, bright, piquante, small, almost the twin of her namesake in *Oldbury ;* and Zebée, the cheerful burden-bearer, with her mobile, tender, brave, prophetic face, in her nature akin to Ruth in Annie's first novel, *Through the Shadows ;* and Fanny, the one determined pedant of the school. Fanny, who was thought a little odd by most of her companions, and never seemed to fit in properly anywhere, made a lasting impression on Annie's mind, though the friendship between them did not extend beyond school days. There is a remembrance of Fanny's quaint, slight figure, and self-regardless manner, clouded over by sudden fits of shamefacedness, of the keen brain, so heavily weighted with knowledge, as one realised, through the symbol of that actual large head set upon the slim neck, so much too heavy for it to bear—a remembrance that gleams out here and there in many persons and places through Annie's writings; in Mildred, of *A Doubting Heart*, for example; in Mary Bourdillon, in *A York and a Lancaster Rose;* a little even in the Janet of *Janet's Home.* Annie knew the characters of all her girl friends and acquaintances, imaginatively and sympathetically. Her imaginative reading of character gave her that faculty of insight which awakens sympathy, and works by the force of love, which sees the things that are not—not yet, that is to say, apparent—and calls them as though they were, because it sees that they are potentially there, and will some day appear. It was always the potential good that Annie saw; it was revealed as by a lightning-flash to her loving heart, and never faded from it again. She never saw the worst side of others chiefly, or first, or indeed at all. One could not persuade her that any one was out and out base, hypocritical, unworthy. I do not think I can remember her ever feeling any one to be distinctly repugnant to her. Yet this beautiful habit of mind was capable of becoming tiresome to more prosaic natures, to such as never penetrate deeper than into the region of righteousness. To one who puts himself in the attitude of a judge, it cannot fail to feel tiresome that the faults of others, those torturing motes which chafe the spirit of condemnation, cannot get recognition of their existence at all; but Annie's understanding gentleness was always strong to help

and full of healing power to the soul that knew
itself, and stumbled beneath the weight of its own
burden.

There was one condition of her school-life out
of which Annie drew much pleasure. Every elder
girl at the school was invited to adopt one of the
younger children, who became henceforth her special
charge. The girl took the place of mother to the
child, taught her her lessons in preparation hours,
superintended her plays, made herself the referee in
all difficulties. The most motherly girls were sometimes allowed to adopt more than one child. There
were many who loved to call Annie "mother."
The very troublesome children generally came to her
share, those whom everybody else had tried, and been
tired out by; and she loved them quite as well as if
they had been so many cherubs. It might seem to
outsiders that they imposed upon her good nature,
but, after all, the unruly spirits did grow tamer with
her, and the weakly ones stumbled less often in her
company. It was astonishing how many good points
came to the front, how teachers and scholars alike
began to hope again where she had first believed.

Annie had many pleasant recollections of her
school-days; of long, happy communings with friends
in the pretty, shaded avenue of the garden, or whilst
walking up and down its broad sunny walk, skirted
by rows of old-fashioned moss and cabbage rose-
trees; of the holidays, the children's days, when
little groups and families settled themselves in
pleasant nooks for story-telling and talk, or

played, once in a way, uproarious, merry games upon the grass.

Life at home when Annie came back to it was not exactly in a bright stage, but still it was family life more really than it had been in her dream-child-hood, and she found much quiet happiness in it. Nothing like gaiety came near her, and there was little enjoyment of society outside the home-circle. It was a life which would have been thought very dull by most girls, but Annie never found it so, for her intellectual life was too vivid to need outward excitement or stimulus. She read a great deal; her education may be said to have begun then; and her thoughts occupied themselves upon many subjects.

The person she looked up to most in her youth, and who influenced her opinions and her tastes more than any one else did, was her brother Henry, the next but one to her in age, and two years older than her playmate-brother Arthur.

Henry was in the midst of a distinguished college career about the time when Annie returned from school, and he spent many of his vacations at home, bring-ing with him always some new interest or idea which Annie delighted to discuss with him. This brother Henry became from that period of her life a sort of ideal to her, and she more earnestly desired his good opinion than that of any one else. The brother and sister were at the same time alike and unlike, alike in root, one might say, and unlike in fruit; most alike when very young, before either was fully developed. The great meeting-ground between them was imagination; but whilst Annie's imagination seemed a part of every part of her, in Henry, imagination chiefly influenced the moral region. Henry, though highly gifted in many ways, was not an inventor of any kind. He had not even any great admiration for originality in others, and had no artistic bias, but he was enthusiastic in his appreciation of all that was great, or good, and thrilled with pleasure at the record of any simple, noble deed. He was what Annie used to call extremely *real*, and was never ashamed of being so. He was not suspicious of enthusiasms; true and simple himself, and very much in earnest, he easily believed in the genuineness of feeling in others. Annie found great pleasure in the unreservedness of his nature, for Henry was remarkably free from that sort of personal pride which sometimes clouds over really fine characters, making it impossible to some persons to acknowledge themselves in the wrong, or to make amends for injuries done. Henry could always quite frankly say, "I have been to blame, forgive me." He became humble to *any* one the moment he saw that he had given pain, even by a hasty word, and Annie was exactly like him in this, if possible, more quickly conscious even than he was of any little unkind word said, and more anxious to make amends for it. Singularly just in their appreciation of the rights of others, they were both ready to the instant with such sacrifices of self. As Henry grew older he became a little sterner in his morality; having trusted fully, he

was proportionally disappointed when he found himself mistaken; there were no half courses with
him, if he admired warmly, he condemned strongly.
Annie was, as we have seen, positively unable to see
any one in deep shadow; condemnation was foreign
to her nature; her mind was more subtle, her feelings were more complex than her brother's, so that
there was sometimes a difference though never a
discord between them; he was apt to be disappointed
at her halting judgments, her cloudiness of vision
about the faults of those dear to her, which looked
simply like untruthfulness in his eyes, whilst on the
other hand her hunger for his perfectly approving
love was never in this world fully satisfied.

Yet Henry remained one of Annie's ideals, and
she was always prone to appreciate in men those
fine points which had first attracted her in him.

Two or three years passed quietly on—the opening
years of Annie's youth—without change, or any break
apparent in the outlook on any side. On the key
which these years sounded her life's music was played,
they were typical of its course : few events marked
it, no great success was ever reached, it was most
like some soft spring day, fair and shadowed and
sweet, of grey cloud above and gradual promise
below.

Annie never wished for change, she was in no
hurry to begin her experience of life, but at last a
change did come, and with it an influence that
touched her inner life and left everything a little
changed there for ever after.

The family had to leave the old home. The limit of the invalid father's strength was reached; he was forced to give up all work and try what soothing to his sufferings the warmer atmosphere of a southern county might bring. The family removed to Clifton, near Bristol.

A good deal of brightness came into Annie's life during the three years that followed. She made many new friends in the new place, and by the influence of some of them a strong impulse was given to her love of study; a desire to express her own thoughts in writing began also to form itself in her mind then. But that those three years changed her more than she was changed by any other three years of her life was owing to the influence of one friend only, one who came nearer to her than any other person ever came before or after.

It is not strange that in her youth Annie should have inspired a strong and beautiful love, nor that it should have been just her dream-nature, her apartness, her own singularly unimpressionable condition of mind that attracted the imagination of her lover. Love is blind, people say; sometimes it is love only which can clearly see; certainly he who loved Annie read her character better than many of those who had known her from her childhood even. He understood exactly the contradiction that there was between her timidity and her strength; worshipping the ideal purity of her nature and the greatness of which she was capable. He saw, and understood too, how she had to be won by the charm and repose of friendship, wooed out of her dream-world like some rare and shy air or water creature, step by step, until she came to build her house upon the common ground, and fashion hopes of happiness for this actual sphere. He fully appreciated her artistic power, and helped to give her confidence in it, comprehending at the same time her pleasure in authorship and her pain in that shock of contact with the outward world which even the most unpretending writer must experience. He saw beforehand just how and where the hardness of life would depress and hurt her, how unfit she really was for any struggle, what a safeguard tenderness might be to her, and fondly hoped that she would be unceasingly surrounded by it. Little by little, in the small events of life, by long friendly converse through beautiful quiet days in the sunshine of their youth, his love shone forth in its strength, and her affection put gentle tendrils out, reaching towards it, struggling into joy. Mentally the lovers were akin, both imaginative, both speculative,—speculation on religious philosophical subjects being especially interesting to them both about the time when they first met. In such spheres of thought he was indeed freer and bolder than she was ; he led and she followed. It might have been difficult to turn back on such a course, but Annie was always subject to the disturbance of contrary impulses ; for her lover and the brother whose lead she had, until then, tried to follow, were almost opposing influences as far as opinions were concerned, and this was the cause of not a little suffering to her.

The intercourse between Annie and this friend
extended over several years, and during the course of
these years her life was broken in upon by a great
sorrow, bringing with it an unexpected responsibility.
The great sorrow which wrecked the happiness of one
of her elder brothers' homes, was the beginning of a
new era of life to Annie, for she was called upon to fill
a mother's place to three motherless children. No
more congenial sphere of work could possibly have
been found for her; for mother-nature was stronger
in her than any other nature was. The six years of
her charge in that home were the golden years
of her life, in which every part of her was satisfied and her character showed its natural bent then.
The home she went to was a country home, in the
pretty village of Trent Vale in Staffordshire. There
Annie enjoyed plenty of leisure and freedom; she
took in and gave out on all sides, renewing her
acquaintance with nature, and exercising her newly-
discovered gift of writing. But everything she did was
inspired by or turned towards what was the centre of
her life—her care of the children. Whatever new
thing she learned of bird, or insect, or flower, whatever beauty she discovered in written book, or living
action, she took straight to them as a mother bird
carries treasure to her nest. All changes of the hours,
every season of the year, she set and tuned to the
requirements of nursery life; in summer time,
the little garden and the field, the banks of the canal
close by, the bluebell woods further away, had each
their changing pleasures; the nursery, nay, the whole

house, in winter afternoons and in the evening fire-
glow, were no less the inspirers of games or quaint,
weird fairy tales.

Some of the prettiest of her children's fairy tales
Little Wanderlin amongst them (not published till
long afterwards), were written for that nursery. In
writing it was always necessary for her to realise her
hearers, and she never gave shape to her fancies
more pleasurably than she did when fashioning
them for that one child-audience she loved so well.
Of the rhymes she wrote for it few ever saw the
light, but these two express so simply the sunshine
of the child-life she shared with the children that I
am tempted to insert them here.

Fairy Men was suggested by the summer rambles
in the bluebell wood; the second, called *Rocking
and Talking*, gives an idea of the happy twilight
amusements and talk.

FAIRY MEN.

In Trentham woods we gathered flowers,
    'Twas growing latish, when
Tripping between the hyacinth stalks
    I spied the fairy men.
I wish, don't you, that you had been
    Standing near me then?

In jackets green and velvet caps,
    With feather in the band;
Not one of them was half so big
    As Charlie's little hand.
I took my bonnet from my head,
    And curtseying did stand

To watch them as they tripped along
  The hyacinth-woven bower ;
Beneath each fairy foot-fall
  Sprang up a little flower,
And the mossy grass grew greener,
  As after a spring shower.

By twos the merry hunting elves
  Marched first to clear the way ;
They'd lances made of hornets stings,
  And caps with trophies gay :
In deadly fight with dragon-flies
  No braver men than they.

Then came the gentle flowers fays,
  Each one an artist pale ;
Their business is to paint the flowers
  That blossom in the vale :
And though they work by dim moonlight
  Their colours never fail.

Next passed the elves who love to creep
  On children's beds at night,
To whisper tales of fairy land
  When nurse puts out the light :
Each one carried a folded dream,
  To spread on a pillow white.

Last the sad stooping cobbolds came,
  Through earth-holes small they creep ;
With patient steps they struggle up
  The under ways so steep :
For sins they are condemned to work
  While other fairies sleep.

They carry tiny water-pails
  Upon their shoulders small,
Toilsomely in the under world
  Work they to fill them all :
Catching each raindrop as it drips
  Through their dark cavern wall.

All night through fields and lanes they go,
  And deftly as they run
They slip a dewdrop in each flower,
  On each grass-blade hang one,
Yet dare not wait to see them turned
  To diamonds by the sun.

So winding on through Trentham woods
  I watched the fairy men,
The tall ferns hid them from my sight,
  I think you called me then.
Could I have dreamt that pleasant scene,
  Or will they come again ?

ROCKING AND TALKING.

Gently, no pushing, there's room to sit
All three without grumbling;
One in front, two behind—well, you fit,
With your aunt to keep you from tumbling.
Rock, rock, old rocking chair,
You'll last us a long time with care ;
And still without balking   ·
Of us four any one,
Of rocking and talking—
That is what we call fun.

Curtains drawn and no candles lit,
Great red caves in the fire :
This is the time for us four to sit
Rocking and talking all four till we tire.
Rock, rock, old rocking chair,
How the fire-light glows up there
Red on the white ceiling ;
The shadows every one
Might be giants reeling
On their great heads for fun.

F

Shall we call this a boat out at sea,
We four sailors rowing?
Can you fancy it, well? as for me
I feel the salt wind blowing;
Up, up and down, lazy boat,
On the top of a wave we float,
Down we go with a rush;
Far off I see the strand
Glimmer, our boat we'll push
Ashore on fairy land.

The fairy people come running
To meet us down on the strand,
Each holding out towards us the very thing
We most wish for held in his hand.
Up again—one wave more
Keeps us back from the fairy shore,
Let's pull all together;
Then with it up we'll climb
To the always fine weather
That makes up fairy time.

Ah! the tide sweeps us out of our track,
The glimmer dies in the fire,
There's no climbing the wave that holds back
The one thing we all most desire.
Never mind—rock, rocking chair,
While there's room for us four there
To sit by the fire-light swinging,
Shut in by the nursery door;
Birds in their own nest singing
Aren't happier than we four.

A record of those days by one of the three
nephews may serve to give a picture of them and
of Annie's part in them as they appeared in the eyes
of childhood, and were remembered in after times.
"Annie Keary," this one says, "surpassed any one

I have ever known in her capacity of sympathy with children, and of penetrating behind the barriers which a child's instinct teaches it to raise between an indifferent outer world, and its own shy, eager spirit. Wherefore it was that no children were ever found who could resist her charm; and she on her side found no child whom she considered beneath her interest.

" From her it was that these souls, while yet moving about in a world unrealised, first found a hand stretched to them as from some cloud-covered upper sphere. When children have ceased crying only for food, the next thing they ask is for the bread of knowledge, the satisfaction first of the mere instinct of curiosity, then of some higher spiritual instincts. To none of these prayers did Annie Keary reply by giving the stone of indifference, of false knowledge, or of barren jest. She knew, none so well, how to draw from their shy hiding-places all the best faculties of the child's mind—faculties of thought and fancy which, if dissipated then, or left unnourished, will never grow again in after life : these capabilities, of which while we most of us recognise them as the special gift of childhood, we nevertheless too often forget the delicate and fragile nature, which is the reason why they do not survive to be the possessions of a maturer age. Rarer, therefore, and more precious than many Fröbel's systems, or than a thousand well-ordered 'kindergartens,' is a capacity such as this understanding the heart and mind of childhood.

" To us for the time that we were under this charge,

it was veritably a paradisiacal age—a time all too short, as years in paradise are; for with me it came to an end with my sixth year. Of my whole life, which has now numbered nearly six times six years, this time seems still to occupy a full moiety—nay, these remaining years have at times seemed little else than a tedious afterpiece, where all the light of life has gone from out of the actors.

"The spot to which Aunt Annie came, like another Ormazd, with power to turn it into a paradise, was indeed in itself commonplace enough, yet, happily, with no great obstacles in the way of her creative faculty. That she could (and in childhood had done) raise up a new world in the midst of the dirt and smoke of a town street, I do not doubt, but fortunately the effort was not necessary in this case. A moderate-sized white house, separated by some few score yards of drive from the road—this was the centre, our *umbilicus orbis*. Behind the house a stable-yard, flower and kitchen gardens, small plantation, &c., and then a field, which sloped down to—not a river, but a winding canal, at the bottom of the valley. Beyond the canal the ground rose in gentle slopes till it was crowned along all that horizon by trees, one country house visibly nestled among them. On the other side a shady road, a church almost opposite the gate; beyond the church the village, and beyond the village, to give the needful inferno element, one or two brick-kilns, whose ministers (the *ultimi Britanni* of our world) were evil-looking, dark-faced boys, terrible to speech

or thought. These brick-kilns were introduced into
one of the stories Aunt Annie wrote for us, which
was afterwards published under the title of *Sidney
Grey*.

" Out of these visible surroundings grew a mythic
world, and the chief myth-maker was Annie Keary.
Children can of their own power go a little way only
in the art of invention, their knowledge being
altogether too limited, and their imaginative faculties
though strong for reception being unequal to the
task of creation. Therefore it is that in all the
fancies in the *Aberglaube*, which made up the poetry
of life in those days, I can trace her initiative. To
put on record out of what airy trifles all this pleasure
was built up, will, I know, raise the scorn of an
examination-passing youth, and probably call down
the severe displeasure of our ' Professors of Natural
History' and other Smelfunguses and Dryasdusts.
Nevertheless something of the sort shall be at-
tempted. I think from certain signs that the vision
which first of all rises up in my memory must belong
to a time before I had reached my fourth year. We
are five of us crowded together upon a drawing-room
sofa ; no light in the room save what is shed by a
small toy lantern. This is both a sofa and not a sofa.
It is a sledge. On it we are driving through some
mountainous country—alps I say now, but of course
gave no distinct name to it then. Only this I know
that the darkness upon one side is in reality a
yawning precipice. It is bitter cold. We huddle
together, with teeth chattering through cold and

fear, for hark, there is a dull sound, which comes from the blackness behind. It draws nearer; it is a howl—the howl of wolves. Crack your whip, sledgeman; drive as you have never driven before; forget if you can the gaping precipice. It is better to fall into its mouth than the mouth of the wolves.

"Or be it we are playing in the garden upon a summer's day; and we wander about smelling the flowers, watching the bees, or the ants building up their houses. Nothing here surely can tell of danger. Yet even in this paradise all is not well. There is as it were a lurking Ahrimanes somewhere. The question is, *where?* What think you of that dark-looking arbour at the end of the long grass plot? Who will venture to explore its shadows, and set our minds at rest? So we take hands, and walk nearer and nearer, and then very often before we get up to the dreaded place a panic fear seizes us, and we run wildly back to the place of safety. This was the earliest form of a game which often enough degenerated into the common children's game of hide and seek; but it was an altogether superior, in fact, a quite sublimated form of that game. No one was really in the arbour. What form the dreadful being would take when he did appear imagination might decide as it chose. We called the men of the arbour sometimes giants, sometimes robbers; but we never saw them with fleshly eyes.

"From these examples it may be gathered (what will be a matter of blame to some, but is in my eyes a matter of supremest praise) that in putting her imagination at the service of children, Annie Keary acted as a true artist, and not with a didactic purpose constantly at her back, such a purpose as continually militates with art. She threw her whole soul into the business without reckoning too nicely the less or more; she stimulated our fancies as nature herself stimulates them, to pleasure or to gentle sorrow, sometimes even to terror. On one occasion I can remember pausing with her upon a landing to look over the landscape of a summer Sunday evening (I probably on my way to bed), and how she said and taught me to say after her, 'Good bye, beautiful Sunday, I shall never see you again,' words which sank into my soul with an infinity of solemn pathos, and still echo there like sounds coming over a far waste of water.

"She did not scruple to show us the pictures which illustrated Dickens's story of Little Nell in *Master Humphrey's Clock*, and explain to us the whole history of them, whereof that of the little dwarf had and has manifold terrible associations; or even in Kenny Meadows' *Illustrated Shakespeare* the representation of Lady Macbeth in the act of saying, ' There's blood upon this hand.' That Shakespeare was an infinite delight! How often have I lingered over the picture of the ghost beckoning Hamlet to follow him upon the battlements, or afterwards descending into the earth, to sulphurous and tormenting fires; or over the fairy forms in the *Tempest*, or *Midsummer Night's Dream ;* or again, over Falstaff, and Prince

Hal and Harry Hotspur. Long before we had read
a word of Shakespeare, Hotspur and Henry the Fifth
were the most favourite of all favourite heroes, and
the continual subjects of impersonation in our make-
believes of adventure.

"Special occasions, such as birthdays (or it might
sometimes only be a very wet afternoon), were made
the opportunities for more elaborate games, in which
many members of the household were engaged to
take a part. These plays, like most of the others,
were of a character which appealed strongly to the
imagination. Indeed they only emphasised with an
impressiveness of scenal arrangement the beliefs
which were the common constituents of our world.
They performed the part which the striking cere-
monies of modern religions, or which the mysteries
and dramas of the heathen world, were designed to
take. One among these great functions of the
nursery was the visit to Mrs. Calkill, a kind of queen
of the fairies, yet with something witch-like about
her, who had been created long before by another
head and in another nursery.[1] I can only remember
once or twice enjoying that treat (only quite distinctly once), but can very well recall the sensations
which attended it, and can still wonder at the nice
balance which belief and unbelief kept in my mind
throughout. There is some difference between a
case like this and those which arise in the ordinary
course of a child's invention. The games which they
themselves invent are necessarily only a matter of

[1] See *ante*, p. 14.

make-believe. Their mythic world exists through the force of their own will, and that will prevents them from criticising their feelings, although all the time they secretly feel that they will not bear criticism. On this occasion my critical faculty was pretty well awake. Yet at the end of all I was by no means sure what had been the real result of my adventures. Had I really been let down through a narrow opening, or was this trap-door nothing else than a drawing-room chair, out of which the seat had been taken ? Were those steps, which certainly did feel cold and clammy, positively the way to an under-ground kingdom, or only the steps of the cellar? Did that trickling water find its way from far-off regions of the upper air into the cavern to which I had come, or was it after all nothing else than the water-tap in the yard, &c. ? Some ill-advised tones from the common world, as of servants' voices in the kitchen, came to fight upon the side of scepticism, or I scarcely believe but that belief would have gained a complete victory. At the end, in a dimly lighted room, our eyes were unbandaged, and Aunt Annie, disguised as Mrs. Calkill, presented us with a piece of sugared bread, or such like sweet reward of enterprise.

" With the ideas upon education at present in vogue there is much in the picture which I have drawn in little sympathy. I am quite sure that Annie Keary's opinions upon the subject of education must appear heterodox if they are to be judged by the standard of those notions which have gained such general

currency among us now. She had not an eye constantly turned towards future examinations. To the
end of her life she never could be got to look with
any favour upon those Liebig's extracts of knowledge
which are designed to make smooth the way to
examinations. If she felt intolerance toward anything it was toward the series of primers which in
ever-increasing numbers she saw flooding the world
of literature; and she would often say that she
would rather a child were taught to think in one
language than to talk in half a dozen. I can imagine
that she was not unwilling to allow those whose
future she cared for to go somewhat handicapped
into the race for life. Nevertheless her efforts were
not solely directed to the stimulating of the imagination, least of all to such stimulus in neglect of the
powers of observation. If those who were with her
did not reap the benefits of this last kind of teaching
as much as they might well have done, the fault lay
with themselves alone. She delighted especially in
natural history, and in telling stories of its wonders,
as of how the mason-bee built his house of stones
and mud; of how wasps papered their underground
homes with paper made of wood-fibres, or varnished
their hanging cells to make them waterproof.

"Some of these pictures have been preserved in the
story of *Little Wanderlin*. I believe that almost the
first time I ever passed beyond the limits of the
garden (I was less than four at the time), was when
on one occasion she took me down to the canal to see
the gnats rising up out of their tiny boats. And

(alas !) perhaps of all the wonders of insect life which I have in my lifetime had the opportunity of perusing, this is almost the only one with which my memory is furnished."

Speculation on religious subjects for the most part slept in Annie's mind during these years of active work; time also was making hoped-for things seem nearer, and as life began to wear a more tender and serious aspect, she felt little eagerness to over-turn. There were points, however, upon which anxiety having been awakened could not be laid to rest at will. The greatest help she got towards clearing away these difficulties was from the writings of Professor Maurice and Mr. Kingsley. With the latter she had the privilege of a short corre-spondence on the subject, which of all others had disturbed her most, that namely of eternal punish-ment. The doctrine of an eternal hope was only just beginning to be talked about then amongst Church people, almost all the orthodox holding strongly the opposite view. Mr. Kingsley's beautiful wórds in the sympathising answer he sent to her reached Annie like a bridge of light across the dark-ness. His opinions sounded wonderfully bold then ; but Annie at once accepted the comfort for which she had longed so much. A cloud seemed to be rolled away from her vision of God, she was able to look up with confidence and trace a Father's image everywhere. The spirit of what began to be called the Broad Church School was particularly congenial

to her at that time : it seemed to take away the curse
from the world, and lift mankind out of the darkness
into the light, to give free scope to human sympathies,
whose every impulse the young had been taught to
condemn by the ascetic evangelical teaching of the
past. It made Annie very happy to have a beautiful idea of God, which she might present to her
children, and to be able to speak to them of the
natural order of the world as being worthy and right,
and leading on to other orders more beautiful and
worthier still. No wonder that the new and healthier
doctrines concerning life and death, and judgment
to come, found ready admittance into a mind prepared as Annie's had been to receive them. They
cleared her mental vision, and prepared her for
deeper knowledge of God, but the spiritual force
which she obtained then, though it made sunshine
through all her happy time, did not prove strong
enough to pierce the clouds of sorrow when later on
they closed round her, nor warm enough to cherish a
heart bereaved of its possessions, nor firm enough to
sustain tired footsteps along the cheerless paths of
life, nor profound enough to sound the depths of
spiritual need for a soul tossed upon that inner sea
where deep calls unto deep through a darkness as of
the grave. .

To these, the happiest years of Annie's life,
succeeded the least happy. Her calm was broken
into by the illness and death of her childhood's dear
first companion, her brother Arthur ; but she was able
to lay aside her own selfish regrets when his suffer-

ings came to an end, and she could think of him at peace, gentle as he had ever been, mirthful as he had been used to be, glad in the sunshine of God. The second sorrow, which followed quickly after the first, was more difficult to bear, and with it her will could not reconcile itself. Her childhood's companion had left her side without withering from her heart or her life ; but when Henry was taken there came with his departure a sense of loss that made an entire separation in her life between its past and its future. Annie never saw any one else whose character she so entirely admired as she did that of her brother Henry, nor one whose esteem she so passionately coveted as she did his; she lost a living standard of right when she lost him, and found herself short of one of her chief aims in life. In a sense she never recovered from this bereavement, though at the time she only seemed to draw more closely to the treasures that were left. But, one by one, others were threatened or taken away. First there grew up anxiety about the health of the friend who was dearer to her than any other, and clouds began to gather over the prospect of her future years; then the change came on account of which Annie as the mother was not needed any more, and a new life in a new place had to be sought out and taken up. She felt this going forth as a being driven out of Paradise ; it was the end of the only time in her life in which all her natural instincts were satisfied, and when she said good-bye to the home in the valley, protected by its low surrounding hills, in its sheltered beauty, a

symbol of peace, she took leave also of her own life's
sunshine and peace for many years to come.

One of the prettiest of her nursery rhymes, " The
Last Day of Flowers," was written upon the last day
she spent in the place.   It was after taking a.long
loving look at the little meadow near the house
one evening in June that she wrote it, and there is
a ring of sadness in the piece which suggests the
current of her thoughts—how she was remembering
other summer days, and looking back regretfully to
the fun of hay-making she had shared so often with
the children there.   True to her habit of many years
she tuned her sadness, as she had been wont to tune
her joy, to the notes of nursery music.

THE LAST DAY OF FLOWERS.

Brother, before we go to bed,
Let's run to the meadow gate
And pull a bunch of cuckoo flowers,
To-morrow 'twill be too late ;
For John says he must mow the grass
Before the sun is high.
I wonder do the flowers know
That to-morrow they must die ?

All day to-morrow you and John,
Will toss out in the sun,
Dead flowers and faded grass together :
You'll only think of the fun,
But I shall feel a little sad,
For you know I always say
That the glory of the year is gone
When the flowers are cut away.

When all the pleasant meadow-lands
Are bare, and still, and green,
They never look so bright to me
As in the spring they've been.
I like to see the meadow-sweet
In the wind move to and fro ;
Purples growing high in the grass,
Red pimpernels below.

Brightly the stitchwort star-flowers shine,
Yet surely if I were near,
In every flower's heart I should find
Hidden a glittering tear ;
And, see ! the poppies near the hedge
Each slowly bends its head ;
Can they be telling one another,
" To-morrow you'll be dead " ?

I shall not join the hay-making
Or play i' the hay with you ;
I am so sorry for the flowers
We have loved the summer through :
I'm glad the sun shone out so warm,
That sweetly passed the hours,
And that the air was bright and still
On the last day of flowers.

" This has been a quiet, happy year," Annie wrote
to a friend between the time of her brother Henry's
death and that of her leaving the children, " and
lately there have been so many sad events in our
family that it seems a great thing to look back on a
whole year that has not been disturbed by any great
sorrow. I wonder whether you feel the same pain as
I do in looking back on the gradual slipping away of
time. I have been feeling it just now so vividly ; I

was looking out of the window, and I observed that
the great trees before the house had put on their
dark green summer colour, that the delicate spring
freshness was gone ; and I felt that another spring
was completely past and another summer rapidly
going, and I thought that the youth and spring of
my life was past, and I took just one look through
its possible summer and autumn and winter, and it
seemed a dark path to be travelling down. I don't
often indulge such morbid thoughts, but I tell them
to you because it was this train of thought that made
me resolve on writing to you this morning. Your
face rose up in my mind with the look of peace upon
it that it always wears in my recollection of you, and
I thought how much I should like to talk to you
about this pain, and ask if you had ever felt it,
and how you conquered it. Don't think I am a
melancholy person, I have generally very high spirits,
but there is such an awful reality to me about everything, especially in the idea of anything being past
irrevocably.

*   *   *   *   *

"There is one other part of your letter I should
like to talk about, and that is, where you speak of
the love of friends who do not often meet or hear of
each other ; realising with respect to the living the
Communion of Saints. I was very glad of that
thought. I go on saying in the Creed that I believe
in the Communion of Saints, and yet I have not
at all a clear idea of what it is that I believe
about it."

Sorrow following upon sorrow after the deaths of her two brothers and after her separation from the children had taken place, there came another change in Annie's life which was the cause of still greater suffering to her than any which she had yet endured. The connection was broken between herself and her lover, and that communion which had so enriched her youth came to an end. Then had to be blotted out an image which through the greater part of her busy practical years she had kept in her mind—of a home that would some day be hers, one in which perfect understanding, and perfect friendship, and equal work and love and care, should fulfil her idea of perfect peace on earth. It was like drifting away from a pleasant haven into a region of storms. Annie was not naturally given to strong emotion of any kind, but she had great tenacity of affection; for her it was use chiefly that made life beautiful. A long inward conflict began then. Then it was that she felt her feet failing where she had hoped they firmly stood: it was then that calling for strength and comfort from above she was unable to obtain what she sought; that the light was clouded, and that she felt no hand stretched out to her through the darkness, finding herself spirit-blind in the sphere whose mysteries she was not then accustomed to unravel.

Perhaps it had been foreknowledge of disappointment that had made her shelter herself so long amongst the mists of dreaming that had concerned always the lives of others, and had borne no reference

G

to her own. After her awakening she never found
the old shelter quite sufficient to hide the world from
her any more; to that extent her experience of life
had changed her.   With Annie, however, the excess
and disturbance of grief could not last very long,
for it was a sort of necessity to her dutifully to adapt
herself to the conditions by which she was surrounded.
She was forced to build up a home somewhere in the
outward, or the inward, as the case might be.   The
storm had passed over her and the flowers of her life
had been broken, but the sweetness of her nature
asserted itself still through her pain, rising up to the
surface, gleaming out in every look and word and
action, like the sun's rays in spring-time falling upon
a snow-covered plain, coaxing its hidden flowers up
again into the light.

Upon leaving the Staffordshire home in 1854,
Annie, with her father and mother and sister, went
to live in London, in the Addison Road, Kensington.
For two years after coming there Annie had still her
father to minister to. She was his dearest companion
through that time, his thoughts of her and his hopes
for her making the last gleams of natural sunshine
about his heart. He took the greatest interest in the
beginning of her literary career. His own life's work
was finished; the books he had written were
already almost forgotten; for himself he had long
ceased to have a thought connected with any earthly
thing, but he thought a great deal of what the future
might have in store for his child, and hoped that her
gift might make her happy when he was gone.

Her father's death was the last sorrow of Annie's sorrowful years. After that came a long stretch of uneventful time. She remained with her mother and sister in the same London home, and there she enjoyed the society of relations and a small circle of friends. There was little variety during the first years of this period of her life, and scarcely any opportunities for self-development or for work; yet she seemed to be able to live in several different regions, energetic and sympathising in each, retaining her own individuality through all. Looking back, one sees how steadily interests developed round her, how friends increased, how affection for them deepened, how rich the time grew to be that had looked poor at first.

It never seemed to put Annie out of sympathy with the fulness of the life of others that her own life had been forced into a narrow channel; no faintest touch of bitterness found standing-room in her heart. Sorrow did not age her either, nor diminish in the least her power of understanding the thoughts and feelings of young people. No young girl was ever afraid to tell her love-story to her; no aspirant after authorship felt shame in confiding to her the most imperfect beginning; ready as she ever was with just the comprehending, wise, enlightening word that gave hope or patience to the disturbed heart, or the unreasonable desire.

PART III.

THE fifteen years which lay between her father's death and her mother's were Annie's intellectually active years, during which she fell by degrees into the serious work of authorship. The old dream-world seemed very beautiful to her still, when, turned back from the action of life, she took refuge in it once more—a joyful world of imagination whose day-light never faded, and where there was spring-time all the year, as in the garden of Alcinous, or in that grove of the Norse spring goddess, Iduna, which Annie describes in one of her children's books. "It stood on the south side of the hill and was called 'Always Young,' because nothing that grew there could ever decay or become the least bit older than it was on the day when Iduna entered it. The trees wore always a tender light green colour, as the hedges do in spring; the flowers were mostly half opened, and every blade of grass bore always a trembling, glittering drop of early dew. Brisk little winds wandered about the grove, making the leaves dance from morning till night, and swaying backwards and forwards the heads of the flowers. 'Blow away,' said the leaves to the wind, 'for we shall never be tired.' 'And you will never be old,' said the winds in answer, and then the birds took up the chorus and sang, 'Never tired and never old.'"

"Iduna," the story goes on to say, "the mistress of the grove, was fit to live among young birds and tender leaves and spring flowers."

It was from living so much in that grove of hers, like Iduna, that Annie remained always young in heart, yet, as we have said, it was not quite the place of rest to her it had been used to be, never again merely a golden mist of feeling, dream, and wonder.

Annie began her literary career with that up-springing of the heart which all young people are capable of after grief. The first shaping of her tales was especially a happiness to her. The nucleus of these was always some little cluster of persons whom she suddenly seemed to find in her mind, and who, as she lived in thought with them, became more clearly known to her, whose natures unfolded themselves as regularly, according to some inward law, as a flower blossoms and a fruit reaches its perfection. Tales were never suggested to her by events, it was always character that developed plot, and it never seemed to her as if she invented characters. She used to say that her heroes and heroines were quite alive and real, and that they spoke and acted of themselves, indepen-dently of her control. As long as any tale was upon the stocks, she lived in it, with a sort of double life, which kept her, as only imagination can keep people, from the narrowing effects of routine, or the roughening of little daily cares. Yet Annie never separated herself outwardly from any of these, nor grudged the time and thought that she was often called upon to give in carrying out housekeeping arrangements for her mother at times when the latter was laid aside and dependent upon a daughter's help. She made no claim or provision for conditions such as would have enabled her to write more easily, but might have caused inconvenience to the household, never so much as the taking of a room for herself even, or the demanding of hours of silence anywhere. She never dreamed of making her own purpose a controlling power over any one else. On the contrary, she used to settle herself to work in the midst of all sorts of difficulties, at the mother's bedside often, writing there during intervals of talk: or she would take her place with her MS. before her at the common table, where every one else was reading or working, or even talking, as the case might be. It is true that she had a wonderful power of concentrating her mind on any subject, and she had besides such pleasure in her gift that she really was. borne up by it above petty annoyances. I can see her now, coming back to her work in the little sitting-room, as would happen sometimes of an evening, after she had been taking an exhilarating run up stairs, perhaps to fetch some book or paper, looking so bright, so thoroughly joyous, that it made one happy even to look at her. That she was just then conscious of some fresh inspiration was clear to any one who could read her face. In that little absence from us all she had

heard something, or seen something pleasant and
beautiful, some little difficulty of thought had been
cleared away, or some new light had glorified her
dream. It made one feel that there must be beautiful things somewhere, since one of us, at least, could
see them; the sober surroundings took a new aspect,
the quiet hours became pregnant with hope as the
evening wore on, and the hand plied its task until the
satisfied moment came when the happy smile upon
her face said that the work was finished, and set its
seal upon it that it was very good.

All this shows the happy side of her work; but
there would come times when writing was not by
any means all pleasure. The act of expression was
often a great effort to her, she used to say that it
took her twice as long, and wasted twice as much of
her force as it need to have done, because of a certain
slowness of mind which her early habit of living in
dreams that led to no result, had engendered. She
never shirked the difficulties of her task, however,
but set herself to work as persistently on her bad
days as on her good ones, exacting a certain amount
of effort from herself. According as the day was
fruitful or unfruitful, she was happy or unhappy, but
no fear of the pain of disappointment induced her
to give up. On the whole, the pleasure of writing
itself very far outweighed the pain of it: but then
the making of the book is not the whole of the work,
and there were pains connected with the other parts
of it which were very real indeed to her.

At the time of the completion of any work, she

always suffered a reaction, from that uplifting which
contact with the ideal world gives, towards self-
distrust.   There was to her something startlingly
prosaic in the thing done, compared with the doing
of it ; it was as if there came a sudden hiding of the
inner world by the materialism of fact.   There were
two sources of discontent, one in having to leave the
ideal companionship she had been living in so long,
another in the development that the characters had
reached; a certain mistrust of them in the period of
their partition from the parent mind, as well as a
disappointed realisation of self in them, like the
distorted reflection of one's face in a mirror.

The time between the end of one novel, and the
first shaping of another, when any such hiatus
occurred, was rather a troubled one to Annie, during
which everything seemed to be shaken, changed,
unreal, nothing more so than her own consciousness
of self.   She used to speak of the strange feeling of
unreality she had about herself when she was left
thus alone between dream and dream ; it was almost
like passing through a period of non-existence, until
imagination led her again into some new and beautifully ordered world.

If the realising of her own work was almost a
shock to her sensitiveness, the sending it out into
the world and watching its fortunes there was a still
greater one.   It was, perhaps, somewhat rash, for a
person constituted as she was to venture into any
sort of publicity.   She scarcely ever got enough used
to little rubs against the world not to suffer by them ;

even the seeing of her own name in print was something of an annoyance to her, and she never got over an absolute dread of reading a review.

She was always diffident of her own power; as one, writing of her and her works after she was gone, said: " Humility, and an almost suffering unbelief in her own power, were her special characteristics." Her suffering had, perhaps, another root, namely, the instinct of perfection which had been given to her. Some artists appear to possess this in a larger degree than others do; they are impelled by it to strive after what they cannot reach, and are consequently doomed to partial failure and to a constant sense of disappointment. Annie needed also to be assured by a verdict outside herself that her jewels were real jewels, not sham ones. She never could cheat herself into fancying that her success was greater than it really was, however much she valued the kind appreciation of friends, but weighed herself and her position with the same impartiality she would have used in estimating the deserts of a stranger.

Whenever the voice from the world outside seemed to confirm the mistrustful voice within, a slight recoil upon herself began, which arrested, to a certain extent, her progress, and drew a veil of reticence over her spirit which was injurious to her as an artist. It used to strike her almost with a sense of shame when she saw that she had revealed any thought or fancy that met with no response, and with a feeling of pain akin to that of sending forth a little child

and seeing that it received no shelter anywhere.
Sympathy was almost necessary to the full development of her gifts.   Had she been so fortunate as to
receive a full measure of it earlier than she did in
her career, she would, perhaps, advancing towards
her prime more rapidly, have attained a greater one
than it was her actual lot to reach.   Annie passed
through periods of really deep discouragement, when
she fancied that she was but a cumberer of the
ground ; and if she could, at these times, have seen
any opening for active work such as she could have
felt to be like a call of duty, she would have forced
herself to keep from writing any more.   But fate did
not open out such a way for her.

The only change she had during her working
years came early in the course of them in the shape
of travel, and it was provided for her by the kindness
of a friend.

Annie's health had been a growing cause of anxiety
to her family ever since the time of her father's death,
a delicacy of the lungs having begun to make itself,
apparent then.   In the autumn of the year 1858,
when she had just published the last of her early
children's books, *The Rival Kings*, and had finished
writing her first novel, *Through the Shadows*, this
delicacy seemed likely to assume a dangerous form,
and it was then that she was taken, by the friend
above mentioned, for a winter's travel in Egypt.
The remedy came in good time, for the disease was
arrested, and Annie enjoyed many years of health
after her return home.

In spite of all the pleasure and advantage which the plan offered, it cost Annie a great pang to make up her mind to go away from us all. She experienced quite a shock of fear in the thought of it—a shock which foreshadows in my recollection of both, another intense trembling of heart that shook her twenty years afterwards, when she was told that she must pass on alone to another unknown land. She never regretted having taken the earthly journey—her one flight into the world, she used to call it ; and every circumstance connected with it shone brightly in her recollection to the last days of her life. She certainly got all the good out of her travel that it was possible to get, and more than even her fancy had pictured ; images were stored up in her mind to which she never wearied of recurring. The scenery of the country made a great impression upon her, and she always afterwards loved its peculiar kind of beauty better than any other—than any, at least, that did not belong to " home."

In her first letter from Alexandria she wrote : " I quite despair of giving you any idea of the wonders of the streets. Everything is like a story. It is endless amusement to look out of the window ; ever so many strange things are going on. At the corner of our street sits an old money-changer, with his beard nearly in his lap. He has three bright brass bowls before him, full of little copper coins, and he keeps rattling a number of silver coins in his hand. Somebody is always coming to change money, and then such a scene of quarrelling and gesticulating ensues !

The water-sellers are very picturesque ; they have great skins of water under their arms, or else graceful, long-necked pitchers, and they carry strings of bright, round brass cups, into which they pour the water, which people buy for a small copper coin. . . .

" There are a great many people selling things in the streets. Boys, with bare brown legs, indescribably dusty, and dressed in a single wide blue garment, followed us to offer us cakes, a curious kind of sugar-plums, fruit, and flowers. If I had had any Turkish money I should have bought some of the cakes ; they looked so unlike European cakes. Women with their faces hidden under a corner of a blue garment, walk along with large wooden trays on their heads, full of flat bread cakes.

" We passed the English church. It stands in a garden, full of Eastern plants and flowers, which would have been beautiful if they had not been so covered with dust. There is an inscription in large stone letters over the porch—' The Lord our God is gracious and merciful, and His truth endureth from generation to generation.' I thought it looked so nice to see those English words in the midst of such a strange, foreign scene, and that the motto was particularly well chosen for the place. There are specimens here of every face under the sun ; from English people, in English costume, riding frantically about on donkeys, with a horde of Arabs at their heels, to the darkest negroes, with no costume at all but a white sheet twisted in some peculiar fashion round them. . . .

" It is a beautiful sight, I think, to see a tall Arab leading a string of camels. He walks so gracefully; his dress, white or blue, swaying about with the wind, such a contrast to his bare, dusty legs; and the camels, one by one, follow, stooping their long necks, and walking with a curious swinging motion. It is quite right to call them the ships of the desert, they really do sail. There are groups of donkeys— quite handsome-looking animals Egyptian donkeys are—and mules and goats, which all add to the strange appearance of the streets and squares. It struck me that the people looked much merrier and better off than I expected. They most of them have such eager, laughing faces, and seem to be enjoying themselves very much. Every one—boys, girls, men, and women, walk and run gracefully; and the dress, however dirty and ragged, is graceful, and gracefully put on; and the bare feet do not look so wretched as bare feet do elsewhere.

" We walked down to the shore, and saw the sun set on the sea, and heard the waves of the Mediterranean splash upon Egyptian sands. It was a lovely sunset: all manner of colours and glorious lights upon the sky and sea. How I wish you could have seen it; whenever I see anything beautiful I long for you, and feel as if I could hardly bear to wait so long before I can talk to you about it.

" I wish that I could send you a little of this delicious balmy air, neither too hot nor too cold, but so clear and invigorating. A gentleman who has

just been here says that there is no such thing
among the poor here as what we should call priva-
tion in England.   Every one, even the poorest, have
as much as they like to eat, and as many clothes as
they care for.   Is it not pleasant to think there are
places in the world where the poor do not suffer
hunger or cold ? "

She describes her first view of the desert near
Cairo :—

"Yesterday we took our first ride into the desert.
We went to see the tombs of the Caliphs, which
are about two miles from Cairo.   I was more
struck with my first view of the desert than even
I expected to be.   I had always fancied a flat
uniform expanse of sand, but it is not so.   There
are innumerable sand-heaps, of every variety of
shape and colour, rising up all round; none of them
high enough to prevent the eye taking in the
immense extent of prospect, but still breaking the
monotony of the scene sufficiently to be a great
relief to the eye.   The colouring, too, is wonderful;
and the clearness of the air makes every object
stand out in clear outline, and with wonderful dis-
tinctness of light and shade.   I think I shall never
forget the scene that met our eyes as we came out of
one of the dark tombs into the light.   The sun was
just setting, the sky to the west was one splendid
belt of crimson, shaded through all the gradations of
deep orange and faintest lemon colour till it melted
into intense blue.   The sand-hills seemed almost
on fire with the reflection of the crimson glow; the

shadows of the ruins fell long and distinct upon the
sand, and in the east, wandering away into the dark,
there was a long string of camels and Arabs travelling farther into the desert. A party of Arabs near
us were just lighting their evening fire among the
ruins; and some lean, wolfish-looking dogs had con-
gregated on a sand-hill near, and were beginning
the wild baying that Egyptian dogs seem to think it
incumbent on them to keep up the whole night."

In another letter written from Cairo she gives
a description of a visit she had paid whilst at
Alexandria, in the company of her friend, to the
Hareem of the Pasha of Egypt.

"I think it would interest you to have an exact
description of our visit to the Hareem," she writes,
"which appears to me to be one of the most interesting incidents of our journey so far. I have so
often read about Hareems, and wondered about them,
that now I have seen one I can hardly believe it was
not a kind of dream. The day before we left Alexandria, the wife of the French Consul took us to
visit the wife of the Pasha of Egypt. We had a
short drive from Alexandria, and then came to a
large white building; the gates were opened to us by
a stern-looking, ugly black man, just such an one as
one reads about in the *Arabian Nights.* . . .

"We came into a lofty and spacious room; in the
middle a kind of transept opened on to it, at the end
of which was a very large latticed window covered
with white muslin curtains. There was a kind of
raised daïs in one part of the room, furnished with

crimson satin cushions. Several girls were standing
about this room when we came in; they motioned to
us to sit down on the cushions of the daïs. By and
by a curtain in the opposite wall was pulled aside,
and the princess came from an inner room, which
appeared from a glimpse I had of it to be as spacious
as the one we were in. The princess is a very tall
fair woman (she was a Circassian slave when the
Pasha married her), and she must at one time have
been very beautiful, but now she looks out of health,
and her face has the most stupid sleepy expression on
it that you can imagine, arising, they say, from her
spending the whole of her time in smoking and
drinking coffee. She was dressed in a very handsome primrose-coloured silk dress, embossed with
roses; she had a little yellow cap on her head, with
pendants of large diamonds, and her hands were
covered with jewels. She returned our salutations
languidly, and then sank down on a heap of cushions,
and began to fan herself with a beautiful feather
fan. Soon after one or two other ladies came in.
One was a favourite slave of the Pasha's, whom
he really cares for more than he does for his wife,
though as with Sarah and Hagar, she is the wife's
slave. She was very pretty and sprightly-looking.
When all the ladies were seated, a procession of
beautifully dressed girls came down a staircase at the
end of the reception room. Each girl carried a long
pipe with an amber mouth-piece, and a gilded and
jewelled handle. These pipes were distributed to all
the guests. You can imagine how puzzled I was

what to do with mine. I blew down into it and made a great whiff of smoke come up, which was not by any means so disagreeable as European tobacco is. The princess seemed to enjoy smoking her pipe excessively; she leaned back her head and puffed the smoke through her nostrils, and seemed quite oblivious of everything round her. Her pipe was renewed about every five minutes, for she never takes more than five or six whiffs out of each pipe. It appeared to be one person's business to supply her with fresh pipes. . . .

"When we had sat and smoked for some time, almost in silence, another procession of girls came down the stairs; they carried musical instruments in their hands, and seated themselves in a row before the princess. At a slight sign from her they began to play the most monotonous doleful tune you can imagine; three of them played on violins, two on guitars, and one on a tambourine. Every now and then one who seemed to be a leader sang a verse or two in a kind of recitative. When this had gone on a little time a party of dancing girls came into the room and began their performance. It was a strange sight, not pretty or pleasant at all. I could not help thinking how tired the poor creatures must be. They danced as much with their arms, heads, and bodies, as with their feet. They went backwards and forwards in every conceivable posture, and some-times stooped their heads so low that their hair swept the ground, then they would bound up into the air. They had castanets in their hands, which

H

they constantly played in time with the other music.
They were all very fantastically dressed, and had
long scarfs in their hands which they waved round
their heads in parts of the dance. . . .

"We rose to go; the princess shook hands with us,
and invited us to come and dine with her when we
returned to Alexandria. Several of the girls followed
us out of the room, and as soon as they had left the
presence of the princess they became much more
lively; they chatted in Arabic, and felt our dresses,
and one of them showed me that she had a watch,
and made advances towards friendship by patting me
on the shoulder. The French lady told us that she
once asked the princess why she did not work sometimes. She was rather offended at the suggestion,
and said, 'What would be the use of my having
slaves if I were to do anything myself?' Can you
imagine a more wretched life? would you not rather
break stones upon the road? The princess looks
thoroughly wearied. I never saw a face that expressed such utter want of interest in life. We left
Alexandria the day after our visit to the Hareem,
and we have now been five days in Cairo. . . .

"The sunsets here are most beautiful. You cannot
conceive how splendid the sky is for about half an
hour after sunset; it is something one cannot describe;
the colours so intense, the air so exquisitely clear
and still, the acacia and tamarisk groves below our
window so wonderfully beautiful in the rosy light.
Then when the light has quite faded, the stars begin
to shine, looking so much larger than they do to us

in England, and one sees wandering lights moving
about among the trees. They look very mysterious,
but they are only lamps carried by running footmen
before their masters."

Her longing for letters and for news of home interfered a little with her pleasure in the journey.
"At last your letters have reached me," she says,
writing from Cairo before starting on the voyage
up the Nile. "I had begun to think that all my
letters were lost, and to imagine how dreadful it
would be if I should have no news of you all the
time I was in Egypt. Write to me as often as you
can, and some of the letters will surely reach me. If
it were only a line to say that you are all well, I
should prize it so much. . . .

"I wish I could come back every evening and
give you an account of all my adventures. I save
up every little thing to tell you when we meet
. . . I dislike to finish my letters. I always feel as
if I had not sent half enough love to you, and as if
there were hundreds of little things that I shall want
to tell you when they are gone. . . .

"Yesterday we arranged our things in the boat.
I have a little book-shelf in my room, which is a
great comfort, for I shall manage to have my dear
books at hand—not all of them at once, of course, but
I shall change them once a fortnight or so, just as if
they came from Mudie's."

She describes her enjoyment of the boat life on
the Nile: "It is Sunday morning; I think I cannot
do better than have a little talk with you just as we

should have between church and dinner time if I were at home.   I have very little to tell you to-day, but I know you will be glad to hear that I enjoy this peaceful quiet life extremely.   It is delightful to go out the first thing in the morning, and find the air so fresh, and sweet, and sunny, and to glide along among palm groves, and harvest fields, and sand hills perfectly radiant with light.   I think I like the mornings almost better than the evenings.   The sunsets are exquisitely beautiful, but then they are so solemn ; there is a sort of glad joyous calm about the mornings that I enjoy more. . . .

" I stopped in my letter to watch a party of Arab women fill their water pitchers at the river, and climb the bank again with them on their heads. They say the Arab villagers are well off, so there is no use in pitying them ; but their villages are most wretched-looking places, even the sheikhs' houses are never whole.

" To-day I am staying on deck longer than usual ; the sail makes a delicious screen from the sun, and the air is so pleasant.   I should like it to be always just like this.   I am in no great hurry to begin sightseeing, the sights on the banks are quite enough at present.   I wonder whether I shall ever be able in talking to give you any idea of what this scenery is like ; I am afraid I shall not, for words cannot express it.   It is the wonderful light that is the great charm.   You will get this letter about New Year's Day.   I wonder whether the dear boys will be with you.   You must remember that I shall be wishing you all many, many happy new years, that I shall be thinking of you all, all day long. . . . . I am almost always thinking of you and dearest mamma. I pray that you may have a happy day before you are up, and a good night before you are in bed, for I am two hours before you in time, remember."

After leaving Thebes she writes :—

"*December* 27*th*, 1858.—I must tell you of our delightful visit there. I am excessively delighted with all we saw. We had a very pleasant and memorable Christmas Day. We read the morning service in our cabin, and then set off in our little boat to the Lybian side of the river. Our boatmen were all dressed in their best, and seemed in very high spirits—they had been promised something extra for supper in the evening; a very little thing pleases them, they are just like children. As they rowed us over the river they sang a curious sort of song. On the bank we found the usual mob of donkeys and donkey boys. Almost all the Thebes donkey boys know a little English, and they all made a rush at us, shouting out their stock of English words into our ears at the highest pitch of their voices. One funny little fellow repeated with great emphasis, bringing out each word slowly and with great difficulty, as if it were a lesson lately learned, ' If—I—had—a—don—key—what— would—not—go—' at least twenty times over. You can't think how absurd it was, his large black eyes staring anxiously and gravely at me all the time.

"We rode first across the plain to the Colossi.

You have read all Miss Martineau says about them.
I cannot say that I felt as much admiration for them
as she did. The first view of them from a distance
is very grand; one cannot see how broken they are,
and their great size and their position—standing
alone in the wide green plain—has a very remarkable effect on one: 'but as one gets nearer the
impression is lessened. The face of one of them
is entirely broken away, and the other is so de-
faced that you cannot see a single feature. I
cannot see that in their present state they have
any beauty.

" From the plain we rode to the ruins at Medinet
Haboo, and with these I was excessively pleased.
The sculptures and paintings on the walls are far
more beautiful than I expected, and the immense
Hall of Columns (all still standing, and most of them
perfect) is magnificent. I walked about it in a sort
of stupid astonishment, and felt that it would take
weeks of study to form any appreciation of its
wonders. The sculptures on the walls are very ex-
traordinary, some of them so beautiful, and some of
them displaying such a wild unearthly imagination.
The faces of the animal, or bird, or insect-headed
gods and goddesses are wonderfully expressive.
You can form no idea of them from anything you
have seen in the British Museum ; they must be
seen together, making part of one great picture, to
be understood. There is one enormous bird that
is represented constantly in different scenes that
struck me very much. There is a strange, human

expression in its head and eyes; and the size of its outstretched wings gives a vivid idea of strength and swiftness. It put me in mind of Loki with his vulture wings. The winged ball (the emblem of Divine protection) is sculptured over every doorway, the wings are always most carefully carved; though it is up such an immense height, one can see almost every feather. Sometimes it is painted in brilliant colours. It is very difficult to imagine what these temples must have been when they were entire, to people who understood the meaning of all the signs and could read the writing. The hieroglyphs are frequently painted in the most vivid possible colours on a surface as smooth and white as the smoothest glazed writing paper. It must have been something like going into a room papered with pages from illuminated books, or, rather, each wall and column was an enormous page, illuminated with far more elaborate and exquisite art than any of our choicest manuscripts, and each illumination was in itself a history or sacred maxim. . . .

"After dinner a Persian with a hand-organ (in which there were two monkeys that moved their heads to the music) came on board. Ellen gave them something to play to our crew, and you should have seen how delighted they were! Their exclamations were translated to us, and we found that they thought the monkeys were live dwarfs, or little genii; and that they were talking to them, begging them to go on when the music stopped, and making salutations to them. The common Egyptians have no idea whatever of machinery; nothing will persuade them that any machinery they happen to see is not worked by witchcraft.

"Ellen and I stood at our cabin door for a long time that evening watching the view. It was a very curious Christmas evening scene. I don't think any party of English children were better pleased with their Christmas treat than these grown-up children were with theirs. When the organ-man had gone they sat in a circle, and the story-teller of our crew began a story, first in a low chanting voice, as if it were something awful, and then getting more and more eager, whilst the listeners sometimes clapped their hands, and sometimes joined in repeating something all together as if it were a chorus. . . ."

"*December* 31*st.*—A strong south wind has been blowing to-day, which obliges us to moor to the bank. We moored under a beautiful palm grove, in which there is, of course, a mud village. We walked·in the palm grove this afternoon, followed by all the women, children, and dogs in the place. Boats seldom stop here so that we are great curiosities. One woman invited us into her house, and as I was anxious to see the inside of one of .their houses I went in. It was very little larger than an English pigstye, but it really was not dirty inside. It consisted of two tiny rooms; one was a store closet, in which the grain is kept, the other was covered with a tattered mat. The woman explained to us by signs that they slept upon the mat at night, and sat upon it by day. This mat, an earthenware jar for water, and a pot to cook in, were all the furniture the house contained. As I left the house a party of women crowded round me, bringing sick and blind children, whom they expected me to be able to cure. There was one pretty little girl who had cataracts on both her eyes, and her mother could not be persuaded that I could not give her something to make her see. It was very sad to see the expression of extreme anxiety on the poor woman's face whilst Hassan (our dragoman) was translating her request to me, and my answer. The little girl herself took hold of my hands, and tried to make me understand by signs that she wanted something to make her see. . . . .

"In the evening we had the whole village down on the bank to look at us. It was a very mild evening, and we sat a long time on deck. You cannot think how completely I felt as if I had got to the end of the world, this New Year's Eve, near this quiet, grand palm grove, and with the rows of dark strange faces looking down at us from the bank. Ellen celebrated New Year's Eve by distributing biscuits among the women and children, and slices of cold meat and bread to the men. Our crew finished off by giving them a concert, which was much applauded by the audience on the bank. The men and boys sat on the ground to listen; the women and girls all stood, half hiding among the palm trees. They would not come forward to take their biscuits; I had to go on shore to hand their share to them."

In her account of her visit to Philæ she writes:—

"Our boat was moored to the shore between the second and third rapids of the cataract, and we went out to take a little walk on the bank. The men persuaded us to climb a hill opposite our boat, and when we got to the top we looked down on a level sand-valley between two ranges of hills. A neat mud village stood on the sand, shaded by an immense sycamore tree and several palms. The sun had set, the sand was glowing with a rich rosy colour, the shadows of the palms lay so still on the sand that you could see little glimmers of gold between the blue shadows of the leaves. A flock of goats, preceded by the goatherd with his long staff, brown robes, and white turban, were just winding through a little defile in the sand-hills ; some women, with water pitchers on their heads, were coming from the river; and under the sycamore tree a man was spreading his garment to say his evening prayers. I was so enchanted with this scene that I could think of nothing else, till I heard our men saying, 'Philæ, Philæ,' while they pointed with their fingers over the farthest hill, and then I saw, first, a little thread of silvery water, then a range of palm trees, and then the immense pylons and gleaming white pillars of the temple standing out distinct against the great black rocks on the farther shore.

"It is impossible to imagine a more perfect scene, it was worth coming all the way for; I shall never lose it as long as I live. We stood looking till the afterglow had quite faded away, and little faint lights were beginning to glimmer up from the village, and the dogs and jackals began their nightly howling and lamenting, and then we went home to our boat by starlight. . . .

"Two at least of our crew always come running after us when they see us step on shore, and . they hand us up and down the rough places as if we were babies. I should not mind going anywhere with an Arab to help me. They are capital assistants in climbing; so gentle and careful, and such pleasant, good-natured people. The steersmen—the boy, and the man we call the Egyptian—are my special friends. . . . "

After leaving Philæ she writes :—

"We are now settled to our quiet sailing life again. I enjoy it very much, and find plenty to do. . . .

"We have just had a delightful expedition to the temple of Abou Simbel; we saw it first by moonlight. It was a most exquisite night, the row to the shore was a pleasure in itself, and I really cannot describe to you the wonders of the temple when we had climbed the bank and saw the four immense figures of Osiris guarding the entrance. They were quite distinct in the moonlight. The faces are really beautiful, though so large, and the whole scene—the immense, high stone mountain carved into a temple, the river in the moonlight, the fertile bank, with its palm groves opposite—was one I can never forget. When I had looked at the temple a long time, we, accompanied by a party of

Arabs, climbed up to the top of the mountain to have a view of the desert. We struggled up through the sand, and were well rewarded when we reached the top. We overlooked the African Sea—the great desert which stretches out for seventeen days' journey without any interruption. It stretched out, wave after wave of dark stony hills rising from a carpet of the brightest yellow sand as far as we could see, looking so solemn and still. We sat down and felt the real desert air blowing on our faces, fresh and soft and warm—a real tropical night air, sweet with the scent of the aromatic shrubs that grow on the edge of the desert, and of the mimosa trees that fence the Nile valley from the sand drifts. I was very sorry when I was obliged to get up and go away. . . .'

" *Saturday.*—This morning we have been inside the great temple. We went quite early, that we might have the light of the sun shining into the doorway while the sun was still low in the east. The doorway is generally blocked up with stones, but a party of travellers had been in before us, so we found it open. It is a most formidable-looking entrance; you have to creep in, or rather be dragged in, feet foremost. It is not, however, nearly so bad as it looks. The Arabs within pull you gently downwards, and in two minutes you can stand, and find yourself in a splendid underground temple, supported by eight colossal figures of Osiris, and by two rows of square pillars on each side of these, richly covered with sculptures. Besides the great hall there are numberless smaller ones, and long passages and curious square dark rooms that look like hiding-places. . . . We have been exploring all the morning; it is a most wonderful place. It is cut out of the solid rock, and the only light that ever could have got into it must have been through the doorway, which must, however, have been very large before it was choked up with sand.

"Since I left off writing we have arrived at Wadee-Halfeh. A strong north wind sprang up and carried us on at a tremendous rate. The country grew wilder and more desert-like as we went on. Now at Wadee-Halfeh, it really seems as if we had reached the end of all creation, and that a little farther on Niflheim must lie."

She gives an account of their visit to Abou-Seer, a day or two after :—

"Before we were up in the morning our boat crossed the river to the Lybian side; and directly after breakfast we set off for a long ride through the desert to the rock of Abou-Seer, from whence we were to see the second cataract. Our road lay by the river for some time, and till we had lost sight of it and the opposite green bank we did not feel ourselves quite in the desert. At last we turned our backs on the river, and then we saw before us the Great Desert. There was not a green thing to be seen, only here and there a heap of very white bones, where some wretched camel had lain down and died of thirst just at the end of its journey. Abou-Seer rises up suddenly from the level sand plain. One side is very

steep, but a path has been made round the other
which makes it easy to climb. The top overhangs
the river, and when we had reached it we had a
splendid view up and down the river where its course
is disturbed by hundreds of little black islands,
which form the second cataract. It was a beautiful
scene. We looked across at the purple range of the
Mokattam Hills; then came a strip of yellow desert,
then a range of palm groves, then the river, dotted
with black islands, where a few dwarf trees grow,
whose vivid green looked beautiful among the black
stones and the turbid water. Far to the south
we got a glimpse of the river where it was tranquil
and blue again—a bend of the shore hid the inter-
vening part, so that it looked like a little blue lake,
shut in on all sides by shores of barren sand, edged
with one brilliant emerald ring. You cannot think
how wonderful the tiny bit of green is here, where
the desert encroaches so on the Nile valley that one
can see for miles and miles the exact spot where
desert and ·verdure meet. It was getting hot by
the time we reached our boat. We congratulated
ourselves that we were really riding towards home,
for Abou-Seer was the farthest point of our journey, and when we left it we began our return.
In spite of all my enjoyment, coming back and
telling you all about it will be the best part of the
pleasure. . . .

"We got back to Abou Simbel last night, and
have had two more delightful visits to the Giants.
Last night was the most lovely night possible. You

can't think how immense the statues looked ; we had the full moon upon them. Some Arabs had lighted a fire in the lesser temple, and altogether I cannot describe how beautiful it was. The first thing I saw this morning when I drew the curtain of my window was the six great statues of the lower temple staring at me from each side of the immense doorway which they guard. It was a thoroughly Egyptian scene. Some wandering Arabs had taken up their temporary abode in the temple. Some of them were preparing their breakfast, and others breaking up some of the beautiful sculptured stones to burn into lime."

During her second visit to Thebes she writes :—

"We went to visit the Tombs of the Kings. After crossing the river we had a very pleasant ride over the plain of Thebes ; then we passed through a narrow defile in the mountains into the Valley of the Dead, which lies between the high ranges of the sandstone rocks. It is the most desolate arid spot you can imagine. The hills are all of crumbling yellow sandstone, with here and there a vein of chalk among them. Nothing green has ever grown in this valley ; it was perfectly still, there were not even birds or insects in it—not a living creature but ourselves. The tops of the hills were, many of them, very strangely shaped, as if they had been partly hewn into colossal statues and then left ; the bottoms were intersected by other white paths, like that we were following, which wound in and out among them and led to the different tombs. We saw the tomb of

Rhamses the Great, an enormous excavation, with great halls supported by pillars, and endless painted dark chambers, in the heart of the mountain. I should have to write sheets if I were to attempt to describe the sculptures and paintings on these tombs. . . .

"Yerterday we rode to Karnac, and spent the afternoon among the ruins there. We went straight to the great Hall of Pillars, and wandered about for a long time. One can really hardly believe that it is the work of man. One could fancy the pillars the stems of gigantic trees that had been turned to stone, and that one was wandering in an enchanted forest.

"Hassan came to me as I was looking up at the tallest row of columns in the centre of the hall, and asked me if I did not now think that these buildings were the works of the giants and effreets, who had lived long ago before Solomon's time? He has asked us both the same question before, and been somewhat concerned at our incredulity in insisting that they were built by men. He thought that he certainly had the best of the argument in Karnac, and so did I. The Hall at Karnac is certainly the thing I like best of all I have seen, not excepting Abou Simbel. . . .

"We spent a pleasant afternoon at the Memnonium. The ruins lie beyond the cultivated ground. There is little left of it but a part of the Hall of Columns. It is very difficult now to fancy what it must once have been. We had a good view of the backs of the great pair from the court of the

Memnonium, but I don't think I shall ever get to admire them. The district behind the palace is the most desolate you can conceive—an immense plain of half-filled-up mummy pits and broken walls stretching out to the mountain. It was once entirely covered with stately courts and fountains and gardens, and for about a mile in front was an avenue of colossal statues, all as large as the gigantic pair that are still standing. . . .

" Yesterday we rode round the place where the lake was in ancient times. It is easy to trace its extent by the mounds of embankment that still run round three sides. One can fancy how it looked when it was planted round with trees and had villas and gardens on its banks, and when the pylons and . turrets of the palaces and temples of Medinet Haboo were reflected in the water. Now it is a plain, green with young corn.

" We visited the ruins of the palace. I made out the celebrated coronation scene described by Sir Gardner Wilkinson. It occupies one wall of the immense court, and part of another. The pigeons are flying away with the news that the king was crowned ; the scribes reading the proclamation, the queen listening, &c. ; on the opposite side the battle scene. . . .

" I went up to the roof and walked up and down, where I have no doubt the priests used to walk in the cool of the evening, and where I dare say they took Herodotus and Plato in their days to show them the greatness of the great city. How splendid it

I

must have looked !   The Memnonium, with its guard
of seated giants in front, and its palm groves behind,
and beyond it the river, Karnac, and Luxor.   As it
is, the immense green plain, dotted with, here and
there, a palm grove, or a group of dark tamarisk
trees, and with the great pair in the middle of it,
is very well worth climbing to the top of the pylon
to overlook."

In one of her journal letters, nearly the last of
those written on the Nile, she says :—

"I intended to have written you a long account
of Belzoni's tomb, now I think I would rather keep
it all till we can talk about it.   I will tell you
about one picture that I thought the prettiest.   It
was a representation of the boat with the soul in it
on its way to the regions of Amenti; it has all sorts
of difficulties to encounter, and in one place has to
get up a very steep ascent.   There a number of little
souls, represented as birds with human heads and
hands, come to help, standing in a long line on the
top of the hill; they are represented as drawing the
boat of the still unjudged soul up the hill, and calling
out, ' Oh, come ! oh, come ! oh, come !'   Farther on,
we saw the boat safely landed in Amenti, and the
dead person, depicted as a mummied figure before,
is changed into a winged, human-headed bird, with
the scarabæus, the sign of immortality, in his hand.
In another room we saw representations of the soul
passing through purifying fires.   At first the mummied
figure stands upright, and serpents spit fire at him ;
in the last division of the picture he is kneeling with

a star upon his head, signifying prayer, and the god Thoth is standing near. All the trials and sufferings of the soul appear to happen to it before it is judged.

"We were able to see and understand all these pictures much better on our second visit to the tomb, for it was so much better lighted than it had been when we first saw it. Candles had been placed about the rooms so as to show off the effect in the best possible way. You can't think what a wonderfully impressive scene it was when we came down—never shall I forget it. The colours of the painting of these inner chambers are as brilliant as if they had but just been painted—brilliant colours on a white ground; and the strange forms of the hawk-headed, ram-headed, and serpent-headed figures stood out so distinctly that one could hardly help fancying they were real, and that we had actually arrived in the regions of Amenti ourselves."

"*February* 27*th.*—We found some very curious fossil shells on our walk; we noticed some others buried in the stone, and sent Hassan back for a hammer to get them out. He returned, accompanied by our boy Ishmael, who is always ready to show his zeal in doing anything for us. He worked so hard breaking up the rock that we had soon a basketful of fossils, more than we can possibly take home. The kind of thing we take a fancy to puzzles Ishmael very much. He is constantly bringing me something or another to see whether I shall consider it good or not, and he looks so pleased when I take it that I am quite sorry to disappoint him; and am getting my room quite choked up with stones, broken pieces of pottery, bits of wood, &c., which Ishmael has collected, in the expectation that the lady will consider them curiosities.

"It is now after our dinner; the men are shoving our boat from the shore; the sun, a great red ball, is sinking slowly behind the distant Lybian hills; the river is dancing in little crimson waves; an exquisite rose-coloured glow touches the tops of the chalk cliffs, the long shadows of the men and of our boat climb halfway up them, growing longer every minute as the sun sinks. Achmet, the devout man of our crew, is performing his ablutions in the river, that is to say, throwing water over his face, feet, and hands; now he has turned to Mecca; he puts his hands to his ears, and bows his head three times in the dust. We shall not get off till he has finished his evening prayers."

"*March* 1st.—We landed near a village and went to see the church, for this is a Coptic village. The church is a curious place, built of unburnt brick. There were several small chapels under the roof; one hung with very rude pictures of the Baptism of our Lord and some saints. A shelf with a few battered books contained all the church furniture. On going out we saw the village school, held in an open court before the church. An old grey-headed man, with a very dirty turban on his head, sat in the dust with about ten children sitting in a circle round him. He had a tin plate in his hand, on which he wrote sentences in ink with the point of a stick, and then held it up for the children to read. The tin plate, the ink-bottle, and the stick appeared to be all the apparatus for learning the school could boast of. The children sat in the full blaze of the afternoon sun, and they looked as thoroughly inattentive and as glad of the interruption of our coming as any schoolboys could have done. The schoolmaster suspended his instructions to beg for a backsheesh from us, and was much pleased at receiving a halfpenny. I hope he gave his scholars a half holiday in consequence. This is the only school we have seen in any village we have come to."

"*March 2nd.*—We have had a delightful day at Beni Hassan. We rode through a palm grove and then over a plain till we came to the hills where the tombs are. You know that the tombs at Beni Hassan are nearly the oldest in Egypt. At the bottom of the hill they look like little square pigeon-holes cut in the rock, but when you have got to them you see they are spacious rooms, entered by good-sized doorways, and some of them having the roofs supported by rows of pillars. The pictures on the walls are not allegorical, they refer exclusively to the actual history of the person who is buried in the tomb. It is most strange to have before one's eyes pictures of the doings, the amusements, the work, the very furniture of the house of persons who lived so very long ago. I wandered about from tomb to tomb trying to bring myself into the right state of mind to realise it all, and to live the life of these people whose pictures I saw before me, cooking their dinners, and sowing their corn, and setting out on hunting parties, and writing down on rolls of paper the number of their oxen, or sitting comfortably in their gardens smelling lotus flowers. All these, and hundreds of other pictures I saw, and my attention was taken off sometimes by liking to stand at the end of the tombs and look through the openings at another picture which the painters and the owners of these tombs must have seen too. The Nile valley spread out at the foot of the hill, the yellow strip of desert, the fertile fields waving with corn and sugar cane, the broad blue river dividing them; then another bordering of gold, and at last the pink Lybian hills glittering in the sunshine—fancy this scene dotted over with palm groves and low villages, camels feeding in the fields, flocks of black goats and white sheep, and blue-robed shepherds walking by the side of the rivers, dahabiehs with immense sails like wings floating along the water, and 'you will have, *not* a good idea of what it is, but the best I can give you till we talk about it together, which I hope we shall soon."

"*March 3rd.*—My birthday. I know how you and dearest mamma will have thought of me to-day. The first thing I thought of when I awoke was your thoughts of me. Well, there is a charming south wind to-day blowing us towards home as fast as ever it can—a delicious wild wind. I have been sitting on deck all the morning reading Tennyson, and enjoying the view. It is only a quiet view now; hills and desert have retreated quite from our prospect,

we have only the low marsh lands of Lower Egypt,
the raised causeways and mud villages, and endless
rows of palms, and white dome-shaped saints' tombs,
and the pigeon villages, and all the sights that we
thought so wonderful at first when we came on the
Nile."

She writes from Venice after the party had left
Alexandria and were *en route* for England—"Venice
is like a dream, or fairy land. I keep fancying that
I have been here before in a dream. . . .

"We have been to see the Doge's palace in the
great square of San Marco. The picture there that
pleased me most was an immense painting by Tinto-
retto, representing Paradise, or rather Heaven. It
occupies one end of the great hall where the Venetian
senators used to assemble. At first sight it strikes
one as rather confused, like a great crowd of faces
and figures with a bright light in the centre. After
looking at it a little time the beauty and the meaning dawn upon you. In the middle of the picture,
surrounded by a brilliant white light, is a most
divine figure of our Saviour; two angels kneel on
each side. One feels that this is the heaven of
heavens—the innermost circle. Numberless roads of
light verge outwards from here to all parts of the
picture. They are thronged with figures, people of all
ages—old men, women, children, youths, and girls—
all with their faces turned towards the throne. Some
seem as if they had just come up from the earth,
they look quite radiant with surprise and joy; others
are seated or kneeling in attitudes of adoration, as if

they were quite used to heaven. Two or three
groups pleased me above the rest : one was an old
monk, who is bringing a great book up into heaven
as if it were the work of his life that he had got to
show to God. It seems too heavy for him, he can
hardly lift it, and he is evidently half afraid ; and so
five or six little angels (heads and wings without any
bodies) have flown under the leaves of the great book
and are helping to bear it up. Another very pretty
group is a man and a woman just flying together
into heaven. The man's face looks upwards with the
most rapturous expression of joy ; the woman, who is
first, looks back at him as if all her joy was feeling
sure that he was there. . . . ."

"We have just been to the most lovely quaint old
garden," she writes from Verona; "I wish I could
give you an idea of it. It was full of very tall,
ancient-looking cypress trees, and at the end of a
long vista of trees there was a flight of steep steps
cut in the rock, leading up to a beautiful old church,
from which one overlooks the whole city. It was
just sunset when we entered the garden, and we
could see the snow range of the Alps flushed with the
sunset light; the church bells all over the city were
ringing for vespers, the garden was quite quiet, and
every open spot not shaded by the gloomy old
trees was covered with spring flowers—primroses,
hyacinths, and periwinkle. It was not at all grandly
kept, and had no rare flowers in it, but you can't
think how lovely it was."

She concludes the letter with the characteristic

injunction: "Get some nice books for me from Mudie's by the time I come home. I want particularly to read Bulwer's last book, *What will he do with it?* and a notice of Miss Muloch's writings in the *North British Review;* but any new book, any review, will be a treat after my long fast from literature."

When Annie returned from her travel she took up her literary work again. She began at once upon her *Early Egyptian History.* It was on the occasion of the publication of this book that she was introduced by a friend to Mr. Macmillan, with whose house she continued to be connected through the remainder of her literary career. With himself as well as with his family she also entered into relations of friendship, which were maintained without interruption until the end of her life.

Annie never wrote quickly. During the ten years following the publication of the *Egyptian History* she produced only *Janet's Home, Clemency Franklyn, Oldbury,* and the *Nations Around;* but then during that time she was the almost constant nurse of her invalid mother, besides being the centre of family and social life.

Some of her letters to different friends will, perhaps, give a better idea of her feelings and of the life she led during these years than any description of them could do. Annie kept up a regular correspondence with the friend who had made her the companion of her travels in Egypt. She wrote to her on one Christmas Eve: "I want you to have one line from me this Christmas morning, to give you my love, and say how much I shall be thinking of you to-day. I hope you will have a quiet day, and be able to enjoy, as you like to do, the real deep joy of Christmas.

"I know you feel as I do that if it were not for that, the outside rejoicing, coming year after year, would have something almost melancholy in it. It is only realising how lasting and universal that cause is that makes the outside tokens of brotherhood satisfying and full of meaning. I write this to you, because I am seized to-day, as I always am about Christmas time, with the kind of dread of anniversaries that comes from looking back too much, and also with a longing to grasp some reality in the midst of tokens of happiness which one sometimes fears may become almost meaningless from being too often repeated. How I long to be good enough to be as happy as I ought to be, because Christ has come to make us all one, and bring eternal life for all. How happy and free from care and full of gratitude one ought to be to-day! One thing I am very grateful for, and that is for all the friends I have. I have been thinking about that this morning, and especially of you ; and I must tell you how grateful to you I am for loving me, and that I feel it is indeed a gift of God."

To the same.—"We have had a very sad time since I wrote last. Mamma has been very ill; her breathing at times so difficult that it was sad to see and hear her. We never leave her a moment alone. I have hardly done anything in the way of writing since I saw you. *Janet* is quite at a standstill, but now and then when I have a moment I refresh myself with reading some Egyptian history, and I have written a few pages of my third chapter, giving a sort of general description of the country between Cairo and Thebes. I find it a great relief to have this project of writing on Egypt in my mind; it occupies my thoughts at times when, if I had nothing of the kind to think of, I should get very melancholy. However, I think the worst is over. Do not be too unhappy about us."

To the same friend, who was then spending the winter abroad, she writes :—

"*January 1st.*—A very, very happy new year to you. It is a cold, snowy morning with us : I wonder how it is with you. Every now and then, after a snow-shower, the sun makes a little effort to come out, and give us a new year's greeting. Then our white garden and lightly-powdered trees look pretty and cheerful, but the snow clouds soon drift up again, and the wind begins to wail, and the trees to swing themselves backwards and forwards like people in pain, and all looks sad and dreary. I hope it is not an omen for the year—short gleams of joy, and much gloom. No, I will not think that. We are, however, sad to-day, for a very bad account has come to us of poor E. P. [a cousin]; I fear she is dying. I have been reading two beautiful sermons by Maurice, and walking up and down the room, thinking, and looking out of the window. I can see

all sorts of things and read a great many allegories
in our little garden.   The two old willows at the
end, and the great solemn-looking cypress in the
middle of the grass-plot, have been talking to me
now for so many years.   I am now half afraid of
them; for they don't say very cheerful things always,
especially not on windy new year's days.   That
cypress does shake his head so ominously whenever there is an east wind; he is the Jeremiah
of trees.   Yet I should miss him very much if he
were cut down.   We have had a great deal of talk
together, and he has told me many pathetic stories.
I wonder what he will say to the next people who
live here."

"*January 3rd.*—I have no particular news to
write to-day, so I will talk to you about the plans for
writing you told me of in your last letter.   Nothing
interests me more heartily than hearing of these.   I
can't help being sorry that the idea of the French
novel has died out of your mind, though the plan
that has come in its place is a very beautiful one.
I think *real* autobiography must be the most difficult
thing in the world to write.   One cannot sit in
judgment on the past till it is dead, yet, to write
about it well, one must take up the dead body, and
galvanise it into a semblance of life again.   It is a
sort of double labour, first to disengage one's self
sufficiently from bygone events so as to be able to
write of them justly, without morbid self-blame, or
self-consciousness of any kind; then to live them
over again with one's *present* self, and make them

real and alive to the reader. I think it is so much easier to throw one's experience into an ideal person. But I expect it is different with you; and there is no doubt about its being a far more useful as well as a greater thing to write a good autobiography than the best of novels. I am now reading two autobiographies, but, so to speak, unconscious ones — *The Journal of Eugénie de Guérin*, and *The Letters of Miss Cornwallis*. Miss Cornwallis was the authoress of *Small Books on Great Subjects*. She was a wonderful woman, and appears to have had great influence. . . ."

To the same friend she describes a visit to Eversley.

" A great many pleasant things happened to me whilst I was from home. The most pleasant was that I spent a day and a night at Eversley. I told you that Mr. and Mrs. Kingsley were friends of my cousins, with whom I was staying at Winchester. When Mrs. Kingsley heard I was there, she wrote a very kind note, asking Ellen to bring me over. She said her children were fond of the *Heroes of Asgard*, and would like to see me. . . .

" I was quite as charmed with Mr. Kingsley as I expected to be, and equally charmed with Mrs. Kingsley. She was very cordial; one can see that she has a wonderfully large generous nature. . . .

" Mr. Kingsley came in, and he, and I, and his eldest daughter went out for a walk. It was a lovely soft afternoon, and we had a delightful walk through the pine wood Mr. Kingsley describes so beautifully in *My Winter Garden*. I was very glad to see this wood, for I *do* so admire his description of it, and have very often longed to see it. Mr. Kingsley's great delight in the sort of wild forest scenery round Eversley was very clear during our walk. He kept stopping us to show us different views, and make us admire different aspects of sky or forms of foliage. He was always looking about with admiring eyes, nothing escaped him. He gathered me some gorse from a bush he always calls Miss Bremer's bush, because it was the first gorse she had seen in flower, and he showed it to her when she stayed with him. After dinner we had an interesting theological conversation. It began with Newman's *Apologia*, and ended with spiritualism. Mr. and Mrs. Kingsley have asked me to come for a longer visit the next time I go to Winchester. I feel I should like to see more of them very much; the atmosphere of the household is just as nice and as genial and high as I expected. Mr. Kingsley gave me a copy of *Alton Locke*, and wrote my name in it. Was not that kind?"

She writes to the same friend the following winter :

"*November* 14*th*.—I wonder if it will make you better pleased with your sunny southern garden, and pretty view over the blue sea, which I suppose you are having, if I make you see how things look here this afternoon. It is a thorough November day, raining steadily through a thick yellow fog. The whole house is full of fog, the banisters of the stairs are wet if one puts one's hands on them, and the walls of all the passages look as if they had had a sudden fright and burst out into a cold perspiration. The only happy-looking things in the house are the fire and old Abé, our cat, whom I have just left washing her face very contentedly on the kitchen hearth. Mamma has been asleep all the afternoon; I have not been at all dull, for I have been writing my first paper for the *Monthly Packet.* I have decided that my contribution shall be, not a story, but chapters on early Norwegian history, and I have got a great many books together, and have begun writing at once. To-day I have discovered in a French book some delicious things about runes. I hope you don't know much about runes, and that my paper may teach you something. I have translated a little Icelandic song in praise of runes into English verse, and I am rather pleased with it just now. I don't know what I shall think about it to-morrow morning. Translating it has made this foggy yellow day pass quite brightly to me, and now I shall walk up and down in the firelight, and repeat the refrain of the song till I get it quite right—

" In brown elfin fingers her gold harp she took,
  Oh ! sweetly it sounded, while from her rune book
  Wise words she read slowly—— Ere one verse was done
  The deer in the pine wood forgot how to run.
          Oh ! the strong
          Power of rune song !
      Chased, they forgot how to run."

· " I find charming little bits of half mythic history which I thoroughly enjoy writing about. There is a king mentioned in a Saga called Fröde, who has two

giantesses in his house, who bring war and peace
upon Sweden according to the manner in which they
turn their millstones as they sit singing and grinding
corn in the mill.   There is a horribly wicked king
too mentioned in the same Saga, who became super-
naturally cruel because he had had the misfortune to
eat a wolf's heart when he was a child.   I delight in
these old stories."

To a young friend, the author of a series of papers
upon some of the French women of the Revolution,
she wrote, "I have been thinking that it seems a long
time to wait till I see you, to say how very much
interested I have been by the last paper you sent us.
It is a sweet and touching record this, of the Princesse
de Lamballe, and one which, as you say, does certainly command a fuller sympathy than perhaps do
the other grander portraits you have already drawn.
Still, please try not to feel *quite* sure that self-reliance
and courage cannot be womanly.   Don't think I am
not appreciating your princess.   Indeed I do, fully.
I am only a little dissenting from what I see is in
your mind about women.   I always feel that women
may be so much more yet than they have ever been;
but they will not, if men continue to insist that they
should *all* conform strictly to one type.   I like your
paper extremely, however, and think it is, as I have
said, a most beautiful and touching portrait."

It is astonishing how many lives Annie touched in
these quiet years.   Children always found her out,
and some of her faithful child-lovers have pleasant
recollections of " Aunt Annie," by which name she

best loved to be known amongst them. One of
them, Stanley Lane Poole, paid a beautiful tribute
to her memory in *Macmillan's Magazine* :—

"My own childish recollection is very vivid of the
wonderful charm of Aunt Annie as a story teller,"
he says. "She had the gift of fascinating children;
she would draw us round her in a circle, and then
begin to tell us story after story, fairy tales, folk lore,
myths, fancies of her own, whilst we listened spell-
bound. It is impossible to describe the peculiar
charm of her story-telling, the quaint humour, the
naïve reasoning, the rich imagination, and the rare
power of bringing it all home to child-minds, which
only comes to those who love children as Annie
Keary loved them. . . . To make children happy
was a passion with her; how successfully gratified
I can bear witness."

With all who had a want or a care Annie's sympathy was almost boundless; she was much more
than merely benevolent; indeed she was not apt to
make plans for the benefit of people in general or in
particular. She did not try to set others right, she
only listened to and loved and understood her fellow-
creatures. It was partly her humility that helped her
to understand, for it kept her from trying to make
others see from her outlook, and enabled her with
perfect suavity to adapt herself to theirs. She put
the glass, as it were, in the right place, and so saw
clearly all through; seeing clearly she judged fairly,
judging fairly she could always believe in people,
and believing in them gave her the power that she

K

had not to help merely — that is too poor a word to express what she did for many—but to save.

Another friend, Beata Francis, writing of her in the *Day of Rest*, says, "One of Annie Keary's chief characteristics was her habit of always seeing the best in people, and, more than that, of drawing forth whatever was best in them. Under her influence people seemed to become what she expected them to be. She eminently believed in goodness, and almost created it by her faith."

In her youth Annie's thoughts had wandered, as we have seen, from the old beaten tracks of religion in which she had been brought up, and she had then found relief from her difficulties in the teaching of the Broad Church school of theology. As years went on, as she read more and thought more, she found more and more to trouble her in the theories of science, in speculative magazine articles, in all that sort of literature that was leading steadily on from question to denial She had not herself any serious doubts upon the broadest articles of faith. Her intuition of the spiritual side of things never failed her, but she found herself warned away in some directions by her intellect from the desires of her heart, and whilst watching the advancing tide of thought, she marked painfully how one after another was being drifted farther away into the gloom.

"It is the very literal, unimaginative minds," she wrote to a friend, " who are so much in danger now.

Their great difficulty is to believe in spirit, and all the discoveries of the present day seem to increase the difficulty to them. It seems as if everything just now were tending to exalt matter over spirit, and to proclaim that there is nothing but matter anywhere. I think the turn will come soon that will set us all right again. All the great questioners lately have been questioners only—destroyers; surely we shall have some one soon to build up. Don't you wish that a day of brighter light, of more fervent faith would come ? If it is coming, I hope it will be in our time."

Annie could not find rest in the place of those who, whilst they firmly believe in the existence of spirit, explain away its apparently lawless physical manifestations; she felt that they could not be the " builders up " of whom she speaks, or give that new impulse towards religion so much needed by the time. The history of the life of Christ, for example, with the miraculous elements in it explained away, appeared to her inconsistent, faulty, powerless, and it disturbed her very much whenever it seemed that she might have to accept it in such an unaltered form. She felt strongly upon the question of miracles, because she thought that a belief in them was bound up with the history of all belief, and affected the value of testimony. It was a poor, despised little door that opened a way first out of some of her perplexities. She began to be made acquainted with the facts of modern spiritualism, by means of a friend who had some personal experience of them, and afterwards Annie had the privilege of getting to know a few of the most earnest and religious amongst the spiritualists themselves.

The beginning of her search into spiritualisn marks an era in her life. I remember the joy that it was to her to get hold of that little clue, and the exhilaration she felt once after passing an evening in the company of some spiritualistic friends, of whom she said, "They speak of death as if it were just a door leading from one room into another, and of the friends they have lost as if they were as near and as real to them as the living." Annie was brought by spiritualism into contact with those who hoped that they were approaching the dawn of a new science, which might, whilst confirming the facts of miracles, reveal in them the working of a spiritual law as real and as predicable as the physical laws of the universe had been proved to be. As the search went on, she was certainly disappointed by the results; she often felt herself obliged to doubt the genuineness of the phenomena; she saw what temptation to deceive the exercise of mediumship offers to weak natures, as well as the danger there might be in the *séance* of letting evil spiritual influences flow in upon our sphere. Spiritualism, it began to seem, was a faith amongst whose votaries one found not martyrs, but many victims. The state of feeling Annie finally arrived at about it is best expressed in a letter she wrote to Professor Barrett, who in an article of his own upon the subject in the journal *Light*, October 29th, 1881, says : " It will be asked, Can we not find a religion, and so rest, in spiritualism? My own strong conviction is that we cannot, and in corroboration of it I will quote an extract written to me some time ago by one who knew much of spiritualism in private circles, and whose broad sympathies, delicate perceptions, and profound spiritual insight rendered her judgment on this question singularly weighty. Miss Keary writes, 'I am very variable in my own feelings about spiritualism, being sometimes as much repelled from it, as I am at other times drawn towards the investigation; but I think I have quite ceased to have any doubts that there *is* an avenue to fresh knowledge opened in that direction. My doubt is whether it is a right door to go in at, whether through it we may not enter into spiritual regions less high than we might attain in other ways —I mean such ways as earnest seeking to enter into the higher spiritual life through prayer and meditation; and whether we may not be in danger of shutting the gate of the highest way by wandering into byeways. On the whole, however, I am disposed to think that scientific examination into these new phenomena must be allowable, and so I don't feel any scruple for such a purpose in aiding any one who wishes to enter into it, as far as I have it in my power.'"

Annie did not, it will be seen, make a religion of spiritualism, but it was a help to her in some ways. She felt that it was a bridge between the present and the past, and valued it because it confirmed the testimony which history bears to the occasional unveiling of the supernatural in the natural sphere, and gave a solidarity to the belief in these phenomena throughout the ages of the world.

Spiritualism did not seem to explain much, and it led as much downwards as upwards, but at least it touched the region of mystery and came within feeling of the breath of the unseen. Annie studied the writings of Swedenborg also, and of Jacob Boehme. Writing to a friend about them she says, "Swedenborg's theory of correspondence makes me much happier about many of the mysteries and dark riddles of the world, but when I try to put into my own words what I have learned from him, I find how vague and shadowy my impressions are. I am reading Boehme now, with the same feeling of vague edification. It is like being lifted up to a mountain-top, and seeing miles and miles of landscape indistinctly looming through tender morning light; one can hardly say what one has seen, but one comes away with the impression that there are vaster spaces and more glorious floods of light than one knew of before, and that stronger and more practised eyes than our own may measure and enjoy them; or it is like standing at the door of a lofty edifice and getting glimpses of the pillared aisles crossing and losing themselves in each other. I had rather—had not you?—be dazzled and confounded by the vast thoughts of such minds as Swedenborg and Boehme, than read the clear, hard cut, inadequate explanations of writers who can't see any mystery anywhere."

Whilst Annie's mind was occupied by these

subjects, came the great sorrow of her mother's
death. It almost seemed as if the crisis had been
reached suddenly at last, for which the preparation
had been so gradual. The care of the invalid had
filled a large part of Annie's life, and she could
hardly have borne the blank it left if she had not
taken up at once another work of ministration that
had been waiting to be offered to her until she could
accept it. She was asked again to take the charge
of children, four little girls, cousins of hers, whose
parents were obliged to leave them in England whilst
they returned to India. The offer was a great conse-
lation to her, and she was eager for the task, more
eager than ever after one morning spent in making
acquaintance with the children. "I feel as if they
were knocking at the door of my heart," she said
when she came back from them, "and that I must
take them in." At the same time she knew that
doing so would demand a certain amount of sacrifice. She felt that it would be her duty to suspend
her literary work during the time that she should
have them, and that this might involve its being
resigned altogether, if the period of the charge
should prove a long one. She did not hesitate on
account of this—indeed she almost fancied that the
sacrifice would be no sacrifice at all.

Disappointments in her work had accumulated by
that time : her greatest success had not been reached ;
she had often felt very weary, had often been wounded
by the roughnesses she had met with on the way ;
was growing increasingly distrustful of herself, or of

having any power to do good by what she wrote. On
the other hand she had beautiful recollections of her
former experience of motherhood; and the personal
influence she had exercised then seemed worth more
to her than any which the wider, looser tie between
author and readers can bestow. Yet when the
moment came to make the final resolve, it did give
her pain to make it. She came back from church
one Sunday morning, and said, " I have determined to
give up all my own work. I have offered it up, and
I feel much more sorry than I thought it possible
that I could feel." Whilst the children were with her
Annie did not miss her writing ; their lives and their
characters occupied her thoughts, and teaching them
taxed her energies fully. That she won the children's
love need not be said ; she gave them a large share of
hers, and when she died they felt they had lost in
her a tender and understanding friend. The time
during which Annie and these little cousins remained
together was much briefer than had been anti-
cipated on either side, so that no break occurred
in her literary career. She was very sorry when
the charge came to an end, when there was no one
left for her to wait upon or protect any more. " My
arms feel so empty," she used to say after the
childen were gone.

The year in which they left her was an especially
sad one to Annie for another cause. During the
course of it, one of the nephews to whom so large
a portion of her love and her thoughts had been
given ever since her connection with their childhood

was taken away by death, and she felt in this bereavement much more than a renewal of the pain
she had suffered when her six happy years with her
children had come to an end. The autumn and the
winter that followed were amongst the most sorrowful portions of her life.

PART IV.

IN the autumn of 1871, the year in which her nephew died, Annie left the home in Addison Road, where she had lived through many quiet, useful years.

During the time that followed, the last eight years of her life, she wrote *Castle Daly*, *A York and a Lancaster Rose*, *A Doubting Heart*, besides a few short magazine stories, and children's tales. Her own personal history during that time concerns itself chiefly with her spiritual life. It would seem as if, at the beginning of those years, her spirit had heard a voice that said the harvest was not far off, and in the beautiful autumn fields had begun to look into the worth of the grain, and turn the ripening fruits all sunwards.

Through every stage of her life Annie's spiritual nature had been ripening ; she had never gone back from any onward step taken, but the mists of thought that from time to time had gathered round her—as in seasons of trial such as that of which we have been speaking—had no doubt prevented her having that full consciousness of the spiritual life which transfigures all our natural conditions.

At one period, whilst she was still young, she had been drawn into close intercourse with one of the friends of her old school days, as she was passing through the spiritual crisis of her life. This friend, Elizabeth, the mother-superior of a Carmelite convent now, had travelled side by side with Annie through several stages of thought. Brought up in the same atmosphere of religious gloom, she had passed out of it to the freshness and relief of wider teaching, and on to the chill that had fallen upon her when she found herself unable to catch amongst the voices of many teachers any distinct answer to the questionings of the reason, or the unsatisfied cry of the spirit. At last, thoroughly discontented with all those of whom she had sought help, she had been strongly moved by the eloquence of Jesuit preachers abroad. To use her own words, she had been converted by their means, had passed from darkness into light, from spiritual death to spiritual life. Elizabeth had sent for Annie at the time this happened, to tell her what she had come to know. The story of her long hunger and thirst after spiritual things, of her wanderings, her emptiness, her despair, of her sudden enlightenment, the rapture she had just tasted, the touch of God her spirit had felt, still more the calmness of certainty in which she rested, was one calculated to make any perplexed seeker long for a like experience.

At the time Annie heard the tale it did not move

her much, but the impression of it remained, and as
her own need became more imperative, she thought
much of the satisfaction which her friend had found.

At last the time came when Annie made some
such resolve as Elizabeth had once made (one which
had led her into fellowship with the Roman Catholic
Church), namely, that she would give herself no rest
until she had found the way in which she could walk
most nearly with God ; and just then she was brought
into contact with her friend again. Annie was
travelling southwards when the meeting took place ;
it was in the autumn of the year that (as we have
seen), had been such a sorrowful one to her, and she
was leaving England partly on account of a failure of
health. The opportunity given by a few quiet days
spent in Paris between two journeys, was taken
advantage of by her to seek the Carmelite nun in
her retreat, and question her of what her experience
had been in ten years of the religious life.
Annie passed a great part of two days in intimate
talk with her friend, during which Elizabeth spoke
openly to her. She did not deny the struggles she
had gone through ; she could not conceal the triumph
which she had attained, for it shone like a glory
through her, and one could not choose but see.
Five years of trial she spoke of, and five years of
ecstasy, during which all realisation of outward things
was merged in the consciousness of the presence of
God, and in communion with Him. Her condition
at that time was a miraculous one, the body was
actually subdued by the spirit. Fasting and weariness

she assured Annie were not only borne joyfully by her, but were absolutely unfelt. Whilst she spoke thus simply of what she was experiencing one felt the power of the Spirit in her ; when she began to expound the dogmas of her Church, the radiance faded, and pain and confusion came in. At the close of the last interview, Elizabeth, almost with the authority of one inspired, made a solemn appeal to Annie. She said that she saw her spiritual condition, that she was sufficiently enlightened to be able to accept true Catholic doctrine, and that she was called by God to accept it. It remained with her to take hold of, or to reject, the hand held out to help her ; to allow fancy to lead her away into endless mazes of error, or to give her reason and her will into the keeping of their only safe guardian, the Holy Catholic Church. In turning away from the Church, she would cut herself off from God. There were souls, Elizabeth explained, invincibly ignorant, who could not accept true teaching, and such might be kept by God's mercy from mortal sin, but Annie was not one of these, for her there was but one way into the fold of Christ.

Annie left the convent to undertake a long night journey with Elizabeth's last words in her ears, and the perplexities of divers periods of unrest crowding her mind. She told a friend afterwards that she passed through a spiritual night then. She came out of it to take up a place of patient waiting for more light, yielding up her wishes more unreservedly than ever before to the leading of the Divine Spirit

Annie spent the winter that followed at Pégomas, a beautiful secluded little village near Cannes, in the south of France, in a house lent to her by the same friend who had taken her to Egypt with her many years before. Annie afterwards described this place in her novel *A Doubting Heart*, under the name of La Roquette. In the beginning of the winter she had a painful illness which prevented her getting the full benefit she had hoped to get from the change of climate. Writing to two very dear friends, she speaks of her illness :

"My very dearest friends, Marion and Sarah, you cannot tell how I have been thinking of you both every minute all this time while I have been ill. It has so recalled the happy time when I was ill once in your house, and oh ! how I have missed you all, how I have longed for the sound of dearest Marion's voice and the sight of dearest Sarah's face coming in at the door. How good you all were to me that time. How sweet it was. Was I half grateful enough ? It has been a great possession to have that time to look back upon and live over again during some wakeful nights I have had since I came here. I have been with you all, talking to you all, and loving you all so intensely, with my whole heart; and I have had a great deal of talk about you all to our dear Saviour, and I have been comforted about you, because I know He is with you, and that the unseen presence of your beloved glorified one is always round you.

"Now I know you will be anxious to hear some-

thing about our life here. We are still at Cannes.
We have not gone up to Pégomas, our mountain
home, yet, for I was taken ill here. This is a
lovely place, it overlooks the Cannes bay, and
has a beautiful view of the Alpes Maritimes. I
saw a little of the garden the first day before
I became so ill, and I can imagine it as I lie
here. I have lovely nosegays of roses and orange
blossom and strange highly scented flowers that have
no English names. I can see from my window a hill,
which is laid out in terraces of orange trees. I don't
know why, but the idea of an orange grove always
makes me think of Mrs. Sherwood's stories, and of
childish visions I had of beautiful things on reading
some of her little allegories. Is there anything about
orange groves in them? I feel as if I had seen this
one in my dreams centuries ago. The gold fruit
among the green is very beautiful and fairy-tale like.

"There are no people in this large house excepting
ourselves and one old Frenchwoman, who does not
sleep here, but goes away at night to the lodge, where
she lives with her son, the gardener. The old lady
is very attentive and kind, and makes us very
comfortable in her French way.

"To-day E—— has been obliged to go away on
business, and I and the Frenchwoman have the house
to ourselves. It is so strange and lonely. Far, far
below, while I am writing, I hear occasionally from
some unknown region down stairs a door slam with
a jerk that shakes the house, which convinces me
that there is some one moving about; between times

there is a great stillness.   My French lady is a good-
hearted old body ; she has just come up unexpectedly,
thinking I should be lonely, to show me some lovely
flowers her son has just gathered.   Now I shall be
alone till she comes to light my fire at four o'clock ;
then I shall get up and sit for a bit by the fire.   You
can't think how I enjoy the wood fires ; no end of
fairy tales seem to come out of them.   I can see
little cobbolds and salamanders and all sorts of odd
things stepping down in procession from the piled-up
glowing logs on to the open stone hearth, and the
dogs, which end not in dogs' but in sphinx' heads,
look stolid and wise over the glow, while the odd
little shovel and tongs look so knowing, quite as if
they only waited for me to shut my eyes to begin
hopping about and talking French.   I wished I could
draw a picture of them for you."

In one of the first letters, written from Pégomas,
addressed to an old friend of school days, Lizzie
M——, Annie refers to her interview with Elizabeth
at Paris :—

"Our chief object in staying in Paris was to see
as much as we could of Elizabeth.   I know you will
like to hear of our visit to her.   It was indeed most
interesting.   We waited for some time behind the
black curtain, from the frame of which iron spikes
stuck out in front to prevent any one coming too
near, and at last we heard a voice behind it say, ' Is
it really Annie and Eliza ? '

"She did not recognise our voices at first when we
answered her, but we assured her we were really

ourselves, and then she unfastened the black frame, and we saw our dear old friend standing in her nun's dress behind the double grating. She was just like herself; not worn or altered by the ten years that have passed, but somehow dignified and glorified by all she has suffered and experienced in a way that I cannot describe to you. One thing I am certain of, whatever mistake she has made—and I do feel her shutting herself up is a great mistake—her errors have not been permitted to hinder the advance of her soul towards God. She has found that intimate communion with our Saviour she went into the convent to seek.

" She seemed not in the least to have lost her interest in and love for old English friends. She was most affectionate to us, and asked warmly after you and all your belongings. We told her about your brother's work at the east-end, and of the ' sisters of the poor,' and she said, ' Tell them we are expecting them to come to us; we are praying for them.' We told her how many were praying in England for Church union, and for greater light and love. She answered, ' We will pray for them all.' "

To her friends Marion and Sarah a little later Annie wrote :—

" I have been long in sending you the longer letter I promised. . . . We are always thinking of you and of dearest Sarah. I can't tell you how dreadful the distance sometimes seems to me. I think about it at night, and I often feel as if I must get up at once

L

and set off to London again. We are very happy here, and it is a lovely place ; but no scenery or place makes up to me for being so very far away from my friends. I felt the same, though less, when I was in Egypt. I do long to see you again, and to know how things are going with you and dearest Sarah. I feel as if it were quite wicked to be here so far away, when perhaps I could help to cheer you just a little if I were near you.

"When I am writing my new book in the morning I think so often of the happy old times when I was writing *Janet*, and you and dear Sarah used to come regularly to hear it read, in the dear old Addison Road. How should we ever be able to bear to think of old happy times if we did not believe that happier ones still were waiting for us—restoration and more than restoration of all we have lost. But for that certainty, how dreadful all looking back would be. We must stretch forward to the things that are before. It is a great effort, is it not? like lifting up one's arms, and struggling to get up to the top of a steep place that hides the view before us. I often think of that when we are climbing the hills here. One sees nothing but the steep hill-side before, and longs to turn back to look at the sweet valley below one is leaving behind. It is such hard work climbing; one thinks one will give it up, and be content with the narrower, smaller view, and sit down and look back at that for ever, but a step or two more, when one gets to the top of the height, how inexpressibly glorious and exquisite the far-away

distance is, where the hills and the heavens meet.
How much better than the valley. . . .

"I understand now why Solomon sang, 'The rain
is over and gone, the fig tree putteth forth her green
figs,' for the fig trees here are the only wintry looking
things, they stand out bare and gaunt among the
other green trees; when they clothe themselves it‐
will be the most conspicuous sign of winter being
over and gone. . . .

"To-day the bad weather seems to have passed,
the sky is cloudless, the sun shines brilliantly; we
have had a lovely walk to see if any of the fig trees
in what we call our valley are putting forth their
leaves. We call this particular valley ours, because
a dear old woman lives in it who has made great
friends with us, and invites us, whenever she sees us
pass, to come into her house and taste her wine, or
her oranges. The whole valley belongs to her, but
she works like an English peasant woman. She has
a pretty daughter who makes me think of Rénée in
Villemont."

It was at Pégomas that Annie began to write her
novel of *Castle Daly.* For some cause or other
she never enjoyed writing this book as she had
enjoyed her other novels. At first she had almost a
repugnance to it, and was so much discouraged after
she had thought through about a third of the story,
that she very nearly laid it aside altogether. On the
last day of that year she took account of her latest
literary effort, and summed up against it. Either,
she decided, the conception was a mistaken one, or

she was incapable of bringing it to a fit development. She consented, however, to think over the matter, and pray about it, just the one night preceding the new year, and then begin the fresh season by casting the story quite behind her, and looking for something better in her dream-world, or by taking it up again and working at it diligently to the end.

She had no cause to regret the decision at which she arrived on the following day; and yet she was never happy in writing *Castle Daly*, and could not understand why it should have been the first of her works which brought her full recognition. Perhaps it was because her inner life was making such rapid progress at the time she wrote it, that all outward shows of things, the whole of human life and nature, were assuming to her deeper meanings; there was a shifting of the points of view, and a difficulty in the re-adjustment of relationships between different sorts of worth.

Upon their return from the south, Annie and her sister made a home in London again, in Bedford Gardens, on Campden Hill, and whilst she was living there Annie finished writing her Irish novel. The circumstances of her life were much more favourable for work then than they had been when she wrote her earlier books, for without constraining any one else, she could command pleasant conditions for writing.

She spared no pains that she might carry out the idea of her story in the best possible way, carefully learning the chief historical events that she wished to work up into her description of the Irish rebellion

of '48, and collecting from books as well as more
directly through friends and relations in the country,
details of the terrible famine preceding it.

During the time that she was writing *Castle Daly*
Annie paid her first and only visit to Ireland. She
spent two pleasant weeks in the west, near her
father's birthplace, amongst the hills and lakes of
Connemara, which she had chosen for the scene of
her plot. Many of her descriptions of Irish scenery
were written before she had ever set foot in the
country, yet they scarcely required alteration after
her bodily eyes had seen the places which her fancy
already knew, aided no doubt by the impressions
she had received in childhood, through her father's
beautiful memories of his home. Annie loved
its fascinating kind of beauty quite as much as
he had loved it—"the frowning mountain heads,
and delicate purple distances, and soft green levels,
shading into the blue of river and lake," as she saw
them at Maam, and along the shores of Lough
Corrib and Lough Mask. She compared the bright
mountain mists to Young Ireland's dreams, in
Castle Daly. "Who can wonder at people who
live here growing dreamy?" she wrote, "for there is
glamour over everything."

Annie knew very few Irish people personally, yet
in *Castle Daly* she has drawn Irish character as perfectly as any novelist has ever drawn it, has even
shown more skilfully perhaps than any one before her
has done, the subtleties which separate it by such
a gulf from the idiosyncrasies of the Saxon. Her

perception of the difference between the two sorts of
character was innate; the impartiality with which
she surveyed them both is another proof of that
imaginative sympathy which was such a large part
of her nature.

She gives an account of her tour in Ireland to an
Irish cousin settled in England :

"We were just one fortnight in Ireland," she
writes, "but we saw and did so much that it seems a
much longer time. I quite despair of conveying all
the pleasant and painful impressions that I received
in a letter. It is a country of contradictions—some
things in it so delightful and beautiful, and others
so utterly depressing and sad. We were immensely
struck with the great beauty of the country in Connemara, and the beauty and charming manners of
all the people we were thrown with, rich and poor.
Everybody was sociable and kind, and easy to get on
with, and the mountain children and young girls, in
spite of dirt and rags indescribable, far more beautiful
than the girls and children we saw in Italy. They
looked healthy too, and must have had enough to
eat, or they could not have had such exquisite com-
plexions and figures; yet the squalor of the dress, and
the dirt and bareness of the houses, were what I
could not have believed if I had not seen them. One
has read descriptions of Irish hovels, but I really did
not think they had been so bad. What struck us
most was the continual recurrence of ruined houses
and villages. Whole villages of roofless cabins we
passed continually, and we were told either that the

people had gone off voluntarily to America, or that they had been obliged to leave by the landlords who wanted their little holdings to incorporate into large grazing farms. The poor people we talked to all seem to have lost all love for their country, and to have no wish or hope for themselves but to get off to America as soon as they have scraped together money enough to pay their passage out; and we were told they do not come back again to settle. Once out in America, where they begin to get rich, they send money to the old country to pay for the passage of the friends they have left behind to come out to them. They don't ever care to visit the old home again. Is not that strange?

" We spent several days at a very lonely little place called Maam, up in the Joyce mountains, and made excursions on Lough Corrib, and up into the Joyce country from there. I wish I could make Katie see the place; she would make such lovely pictures of it. The little country inn where we stayed was close to the lake, and had a beautiful view of an island, with one of the oldest ruined castles in Ireland on it— Castle Hen, the stronghold of the fierce O'Flaherty. The place we were most pleased with after Maam was Clifden, where we had beautiful views over the Atlantic, and of the twelve Pin mountains. We stayed a Sunday at Clifden, and went to a small Roman Catholic church, and heard a very character- istic sermon from the priest. The congregation was worth looking at—such earnest faces, listening with eyes and ears to the sermon, changing with every emotion the really eloquent words called up, and below the faces such rags, such squalor, and a bare, damp, mud floor for the people to kneel on, a pail full of holy water, and a ragged mop, such as you would not have in your kitchen, to sprinkle the people with."

She writes to the same cousin in answer to some criticisms on *Castle Daly :* " I want to thank you for liking my story, and for all the trouble you took about the MS. I am sorry you think Anne O'Flaherty is turning out weak. I don't mean her to be weak in head, or in purpose, but, as I think most Irish people, or, at least, most imaginative, sympathic Irish people are, weak in will, so far as not to be able to force their will on others. She is an influencer, not a repressor. I don't see how sympathetic people can ever be that. They reflect the feelings of all around them too much. I think that is the reason that Irish people fail in ruling when they have to contend : they would be great in organising where all are educated up to one level. They can only rule and rightly be ruled by thought and sentiment. I wish we could talk it out together, for I do so wish to make Anne express my thoughts about the best sort of Irish people. I mean the Thornleys to be the strong-willed people : Ellen and Anne the sympathetic people, who *alter* those they live near not by subduing, but by permeating them with influence ; and I want to show how much more really powerful that way is, though the people who use it often look weak to observers who don't see far

enough. I must stop now, only please go on liking
Anne in faith till the end."

As Annie was settling in her house in Bedford
Gardens she wrote to the companion of her Egyptian
travel:

"You have not seen our new little home yet. I
hope you will come some day during the autumn.
I shall never forget your coming to see us in the
Addison Road, when we first got there so many years
ago. You came in in the midst of the unpacking,
when everything felt so desolate and strange, and
sat down in our dear old drawing-room; and I was
able to take to the room, and feel there was some
interest about it afterwards. I little thought that
I should break my heart about leaving that house
at last, for then I was breaking my heart about
leaving the Hollies (the home of her nephews). We
have both taken a wonderful liking to our new home.
I hope that is not a sign that we are not to live in
it long. This is one of those days with me when the
thoughts irresistibly fly back to old times, and you
know what a large and bright share you have in all
my old times—how much of the happiness of the
best bits of them I owe to you.

"How are you getting on with Harris's *Sermons?*
I am reading some of them over again, and some
parts strike me much more than they did on first
reading. The hope he expresses of some great new
outpouring of love and light to come soon is so
cheering to me; and then his description of what
the new Church ought to be, the love and perfect

union of its members, their intimate relationship with
Christ and the heavenly societies, with perpetual
realisation of Divine presences about them. All this
seems to me so exactly what we want and are longing
for. Surely we shall have more help towards living
in this inspired state by and by."

During the succeeding years many ways opened
out to Annie for searching into the spiritual things
which now chiefly occupied her thoughts; in some of
these she felt herself led to follow, and she went
furthest in the direction of Anglicanism. Perhaps the
impression she had received from the Carmelite nun
inclined her towards that way. She found fellowship
in it also in the person of a friend, upon whose
character and life she saw the benefit of High Church
teaching. There were several things it offered of
which she felt herself greatly in need. There was
clearness of aim. It had often troubled Annie that
she found such difficulty in feeling quite certain
about anything. The real home of her spirit was,
no doubt, in a sphere of truths deeper than such as
can be formulated, but her conscience was an over-
scrupulous one, and her self-distrust made her wish
for distinct rules of life. She found in her newly
chosen teachers definiteness enough to give her
conscience rest.

Besides being drawn to the High Church teaching
by a wish for definiteness, Annie was led to look
there for a Christian grace which it gave her pain
to think was fading away in other directions. It
had been her natural shrinking from their harshness

and cruelty that had first alienated her from the
doctrines of the Evangelical school; the want of
patient human sympathy shown in them, and the
pitiless punishment of the wicked ascribed by them
to the Deity. In the Broad Church teaching, she
had found it a great relief to have condemnation
narrowed and hope extended; yet, strange to say,
within that very liberty a seed of cruelty had hidden
which, springing up by and by, seemed likely to
choke the wholesome air.

An easy confidence had grown up in some minds
that all must be well with everybody in another
state of existence, that the most abject and degraded
person must necessarily be the better for "a breath
of fresh air," as one writer expresses the change of
condition brought about by death; and the result
appeared to be that the feeling of compassion for
present suffering was deadened; less value seemed
to attach to human life here altogether, and the
destruction of it seemed less terrible. The horror
of war which the teaching of Christ appears to in-
culcate, was diminished. The sweeping of human
refuse into the dust-bin of destruction began to be
counted by some as an insignificant necessity of
things, and a large trust in the Eternal justice
seemed to render needless any careful and tender
discrimination in this small sphere below.

Again, the re-instatement of the natural life in a
place of honour appeared sometimes to have been
made at the expense of a high valuation of the supernatural. If human nature really was godlike, how

was one to condemn its impulses? all natural virtues came into prominence whilst supernatural graces began to look pale—independence, courage, pride, overshone gentleness, humility, self-sacrifice. "An eye for an eye and a tooth for a tooth," being more natural, began to look more right than "Turning the other cheek also."

Again, the sense of pleasure that had been awakened in all that is healthful and comely, the beauty and glory of the natural order, had shown itself apt to engender dislike for the ill-favoured, the unfortunate, the helpless. If somebody was to blame that such an one was born blind, then in the readily awarded condemnation the emotion of pity would be expended, or turned aside from the sufferer; and still more this would be apparent where moral infirmity was the cross which the victim had been selected to bear. It was the Christian grace of pitifulness that Annie longed to find again, upheld, in its right place, and she naturally looked for it amongst those whose especial devotion is towards the manifestations of God in the helplessness of an infant, and in the defeat of the Cross, with whom weakness is reverenced, sorrow worshipped, sacrifice glorified.

Annie's acquaintance with Swedenborg's and Boehme's theories of correspondences prepared her to value ritual, and to understand a doctrine which in a different stage of thought might have seemed materialistic to her. There was another point on which the writings of Swedenborg impressed her.

She felt the force of his teaching upon the spiritual nature and the power of sin (something different she held it to be from mere infirmity), and on the solemnity and importance that attaches to the life of the soul upon earth. Swedenborg is not (as every one knows) a universalist, but his teachings about evil in a future state do not militate against the goodness of God. Annie did not follow him to the dark side of his creed. She kept a firm hold on the hope which she had accepted so joyfully in her young days, and which had first enabled her to look up to God as to a Father—the hope of the eventual triumph of love in the salvation of all.

What Annie was seeking more earnestly than any assertion of doctrine or any definiteness of aim was to have a clearer vision of Christ; to feel His power in her heart. Her difficulties of thought had for the most part cleared away by that time; her mind was calm, and in a condition to perceive this vision. One might say that the first dawn—the white dawn—had come, and the sun was very close to the horizon, but He had not yet sent joy into the heart as the rose-coloured morning touches earth and sky with gladness.

The sermons she heard from a parish priest at the East End of London, a devoted worker amongst the poor there, were very helpful to her at this time, and still more so was the being brought into contact with a band of workers whom he inspired and directed. Annie was taken by the friend mentioned above to visit these Sisters in their Home. The first

time she went was on Sunday, after attending
divine service in the parish church, and on that
occasion she and her friend were invited to dine with
the Sisters. They were not the only guests; they
sat down to table with a group of the poor neighbours gathered together from the back streets, asked
to come, each on account of some special need ; the
aged, the weakly, the destitute ; and no distinction
was recognised between the different members of the
company—rich and poor were all equally welcome.
It was like being transported to the old religious
days when such community was common ; and every
thing was quite simply done, it was the habit of the
Sisters to do it. Annie went often to see the Sisters
after this. Their work on certain afternoons particularly interested her, when the poor people of the
neighbourhood, men, women, and children, came
flocking in for help and counsel and friendly words.
She marked the patience and care which the Sisters
expended impartially upon them all, the ready,
unconventional sort of kindness they showed. A
Sister · would go out at any moment, when such
ministry was needed, and with her own hands make
the bed of some sick person, or feed a cripple in his
miserable room, or scour down her house for some
overworked mother.   The life which the Sisters
led appeared quite an ideal one to Annie, and by
and by they allowed her to become a lay associate
of their community, and help them in their work.
The work which she took a small share in was the
care of a hospital for sick children. It was a duty

especially congenial to her. The Sisters sought out
the saddest and most forlorn cases to help—little
deserted children ill of incurable diseases, some of
them, loathsome cases it might be; they despaired of
none, they tried to help all.

Annie used to take regular days of charge at the
hospital, and she never seemed more happy than on
those days, setting off to her work generally with a
large basket on her arm containing biscuits or toys to
distribute, and with the prospect before her of passing a long afternoon in the company of the little sick
children.

She was often found fault with for being a too
indulgent playfellow, and for bringing too many
inventions with her, to fall in with the necessary
routine of the place, but the children did not love
" Sister Keary," as they called her, the less on that
account, one may feel sure.

It was the acquaintance which she made there
with East End poverty that suggested to her the
story of *A York and a Lancaster Rose.* She respected
and loved the Sisters, and the more she saw of them
and of their work, the stronger her love and respect
grew. She said, that in their lives they presented
Christ to her.

One evening Annie came back from a visit to her
friends with a face expressive of deep inward content;
she had made her first confession, and she spoke of
the comfort and strength that she had received. Like
Christian at the Wicket-Gate, she said it was as if
she had left a burden behind her; she felt drawn

into closer communion with her friends, and reckoned upon having always the help of an authorised strength to lean upon.

She writes to her Irish cousin on the subject of her connection with the Sisters : " I should very much like to tell you of this year's intercourse with the Sisters, and where it has taken me in thought, yet many of my impressions are so vague that I scarcely dare to write them. One thing first of all, you must not, whatever I say, think that I am getting further from you, for I don't feel that at all ; on the contrary, I feel more and more every month the wonderful variety of teaching that the Spirit brings to all who seek, and the presumption there would be in any arrogating to themselves more than a very limited range of sight into the mysteries that are being revealed in part to all. For myself, I think I am learning to distrust reasoning about these mysteries—not reason, but reasoning. I think there is no way of knowing anything about God, except through personal revelations of Himself to the soul, and so I *hope* most to get light and help from those who seem, by the wonderful joy and light and strength that I see in them, to have this know-ledge in a special way. I don't know why it comes to some more than to others of those who truly and earnestly seek, but when I see evidences of this mystic union of a soul with the Unseen I am glad, for it is a wonderful revelation to me that He is there and that there is a way of reaching up to the Divine. I don't mean to say that my High Church friends have more of this joy and strength than is to be found among Low Church, or Broad Church, or Quakers, or any other Church; I have seen it in all, and I am not *sure* that this gift of mystical communion is the best gift that human creatures can have. I think it would be given to all if it were. But those who have it, whatever their distinctive creeds, seem to me candles set in candlesticks, to show us that the light is to be had, that it is real. I tell you this to explain what it is in the High Church people I have joined that I value. They happen to be just now the most fervent, loving, joyful people I have been thrown among; and so going to them is always a help to my weak faith, it is like going to a fire to be warmed. As far as actual doctrine goes, I think I do get more and more to cling to and believe in the Incarnation and Resurrection. I find it easier to believe them as facts than I used to do; if I could talk to you I could tell you why, but it is difficult to write on such subjects. It is by thinking about them a great deal that they seem to have sunk into my mind and become truer and more real to me. I cling to them in my heart, because without belief in the Incarnation I should find it so difficult to love God; He would seem so far off, so dissociated from suffering creatures. Then again it is only by believing in the Incarnation and the Resurrection that I can hope for individual immortality.

" Unless human nature has been taken up into the Godhead, I don't see what grounds we can have ever to expect to be more than we are now. I look

M

upon the Incarnation as the last great act of Creation when mankind received the seal of Divinity, took the last step in its long course of climbing up to union with the Creator. I tell you all this because you asked me where I was now. I want to feel that I pour out all my crude thoughts to you as freely as in old times. I am as far as ever from being satisfied. I am seeking still, only more sure than I used to be that the Divine light and love are there, and that prayer and waiting and hoping in God are roads to them."

A letter written about the same time to one of her young friends shows the help she was finding in definite religious exercises :

" I think you will find having a plan and dividing your thoughts under certain heads a real help in the effort to keep the mind profitably fixed for some time on a sacred subject : take either a passage of the Bible or some act in the life of our Lord. I think you will find such efforts useful, and gain from them a real and happy sense of nearness to our Blessed Lord, and actual communion with Him. When one is wishing to love God more and more one often feels as if one was hindered by want of knowledge. We feel gratitude, but love and gratitude are different things. Now I think that meditating on words or deeds of our Lord makes one feel more as if one knew Him like a friend, and were getting nearer to loving Him and adoring Him for Himself, just for being so tender, and loving, and gracious, and beautiful, and for having let mankind hear and see words and deeds that satisfy our utmost longing for what is high and beautiful in character. In that way Jesus Christ comes to be the Ideal of excellence, and sweetness, and friendliness in one's mind, and we can never be chilled or embittered by disappointments in our fellow-creatures, or ourselves, because we always have Him to turn to, and we know that He wills us to be like Him, and will make us all like Him if we ask Him and have patience."

One feels it sad sometimes that life has no resting places, no moment in which one can cease to change. Annie was very happy for some time in the companionship and under the guidance she had found, but because, perhaps, it was necessary for her to be thrown upon still more direct dependence on the Spirit of God she was not allowed to rest in them. Circumstances at last made it apparent to her that she had come to lean too much upon an outside conscience ; she became perplexed as internal and external standards of right conflicted, the rules that she had taken for a help began to feel something like a yoke of bondage.

It was during a short but rather serious illness which she had after finishing writing *Castle Daly* that she became fully aware of the position she had reached, and that she began to fear lest the very means which had been of such use to her might not become hindrances, lest the revealers of Christ themselves might not become as veils between her soul and Him. When in the loneliness that illness makes round one she looked for Christ to be near, it seemed to her as

if a little cloud had risen ; she had been meeting Him
through a medium, hearing about Him, and His will,
instead of listening for His voice in her own heart.
Some thoughts from the teachings of her childhood
awoke from long slumber in her mind, bringing with
them new meanings, reviving old sacred influences.
From that time she discontinued the practice of confession. She never spoke against it generally, however ; but on the contrary, said that she was glad to
have made use of it, that it had helped her to a
clearer perception of duty, and given her strength
for the performance of it.

It was a great sorrow to Annie to have to return
the Associate's cross which she had felt it such an
honour to possess. A break took place in the personal
tie between herself and her Anglican friends, but her
feelings of regard for them never altered, nor was
there any diminution in the gratitude that she felt
towards them for all that they had done for her.
Through all the influences of her life, she was passing on from stage to stage, and always into clearer
light. Her faith was all the stronger for the hindrances it had met with ; her trust in God was the
firmer for the anxiety she had felt concerning His
love to all ; her surrender to the guidance of the Holy
Spirit was the fuller for her experience of the weakness that bondage to human direction may engender.

A history of the development of Annie's spiritual
nature would be incomplete without allusion to the
sympathy of one friend in particular, who was her
nearest spiritual companion during her last years.

Emelia and Annie had been drawn into communion during a time when first one and then the other had been in sorrow for the death of friends. They had felt the same yearning to follow after them into the unseen world, to draw aside the veil, and to know certainly of the things that are hidden. They had been equally attracted by the hopes that the phenomena of spiritualism seemed to hold out, and had carried on their investigations into them together; they had equally suffered some amount of disappointment in the search. Together they had endeavoured to gain a larger knowledge of Divine truths, and to enjoy deeper experiences of them. Emelia had indeed always been further on upon the way than her friend. "You don't know how much I am longing to see you," Annie wrote to her once during a period of separation. "It seems such a long time since we saw you and had our souls refreshed with the news of God you always bring us. I know that is an odd phrase to use, but it is just what I mean. I have so often felt that you brought us tidings from the higher sphere which my grovelling soul only reaches to when loved ones can tell me of their own experience that they have had a glimmer of the light coming from thence, or when I can read it in their faces." Emelia's sympathies were very wide, and her influence was of that kind which soothes and strengthens. It was not in her nature to attempt to dominate the individuality of another, and she was especially helpful as a friend to Annie on that account.

On the occasion of the first visit of Mr. and Mrs. Pearsall-Smith (religious teachers from America) to England in the year 1874, Annie was brought into the way of hearing them by means of this friend. Their especial teaching about faith did not come exactly as a new thing to her, but she had been growing into the condition of mind that enabled her to receive it. Years ago she would not have found any help from such teaching, now it was especially suited to her needs.

The time came at last for which she had longed and waited, the full bright dawn in which she saw the face of Christ and knew Him for her Friend. The spiritual night passed quite away and never came back, and the daylight grew brighter and gladder to the end. Inwardly Annie seemed to be perfectly happy during the last years of her life ; not that she was less sympathetic than before with the troubles of other people, on the contrary, every breath of sorrow moved her. As the surface of the sea is broken into waves by storm-winds, so her heart was disturbed by the presence of suffering ; but the depth of the spirit was at rest as the depth of the sea rests. And when no especial call for sorrowing sympathy was at hand, then the joyfulness shone out, and gave to her presence the charm that brings rest to the heart and gladness to the sight, as the gladness of a sunlit summer sea. " We are almost too happy," she used to say upon bright tranquil days such as we enjoyed together then.

In a letter written about this time to one of her

nephews, one sees something of the rest of heart to which she had attained. It is dated New Year's Day, and begins by referring to Lamb's essay on the last day of the year.

"I hope another year," she writes, " we shall read our essay together, for I remember with so much pleasure the year we did, and I should like us always to be together to compare notes over the year's experiences if we could. I want to tell you of one piece of experience that I found in looking back had come to me gradually through this year, and made me much happier than I have been all my life before. It is a sort of growing clearness in realising that God is Light, and in Him is no darkness at all. I think I have believed this all my life, but I have never, so to speak, known it. I have always had fears and horrors, and always felt as if I could not trust those I loved best to God, for fear He should not be as indulgent to them as I should like Him to be; but now I feel more as if I had got down to the bottom and felt the groundwork under our feet, the substance out of which all our existence is woven, and I can feel, as I never did before, that there is infinite love all round us, and that joy, and peace, and victory, are to be the issues of all struggles, the end that we are *all* to come out into, and this has given me more peace and joy in my new year's prayers for you all than I have ever had before. I don't know why I tell you this, except that I like you to know what is passing in my inmost self; and perhaps it may not be uncheering to young people to know that as one gets older one does really get happier instead of sadder, that there is light opening out brighter and brighter towards the end.

"I have been thinking about your literary career to-day, looking on to the future. It is always such a comfort to me to think of God as the Great Artist, the Great Maker, for I think the instinct of making that we have is, in a special way, a portion of His Spirit moving in us; and He who has given that gift, that *extra* relationship to Him, will not let His gift be quenched, or fail of its true use and development in the end."

The friend who wrote of her in *The Day of Rest*, says, referring to this period of her life :—

"There come before me two pictures of Annie Keary, so vivid and so beautiful that I would fain, if it were possible, reproduce them in the minds of those who had not the privilege of knowing and loving her personally.

"The first represents her as I knew her in her quiet London home, where she was the centre of a happy family circle, reverenced by all around her as much for her sweet and gentle nature as for her great intellectual power. I can see her presiding over little 'pen-and-pencil' meetings in her own home, always appreciative of the literary efforts of others, warmly encouraging to beginners, and as modest and unassuming about her own productions as if she had been a beginner herself."

Alluding to the infirmity from which Annie had suffered all her life this writer says :—

"It would seem at first sight as if deafness must

be a decided disadvantage to an authoress, but I do not think it was so in her case. Being unable to join much in general conversation was no doubt a deprivation to her, but wherever Miss Keary found herself there were always those present who thought it a privilege to converse especially with her. Feeling that her amount of communication with her must necessarily be limited made her companion for the moment anxious to keep to subjects of real interest, and not waste the valuable time in trifling remarks. I think that anything worth repeating always came to her ears sooner or later, and that what she lost was chiefly desultory talk, during which she was free to abstract her mind.

"Perhaps some of her happiest ideas for her stories may have been conceived at such times. It seemed to me as I watched her as though her infirmity kept her just a little apart from the commonplace world, always within reach when wanted, and yet in a certain serene seclusion of her own, suited to one with whom all who came in contact regarded with reverence. Like 'Little Silver Ear,' in one of her own fairy tales, she seemed to hear only the good voices and not the bad ones. . . .

"The other picture of her which I recall, is in a Home for young servant-girls out of employment, of which she occasionally took charge, giving her time with the utmost patience to the smallest details concerning the domestic duties of rough, untrained girls, or the complaints of exacting mistresses; but however she appears before me

in these, the bright working years of her life, it
is always with the same gentle manners and move-
ments, never too hurried or too important to attend
to other people's affairs, however tedious or trivial,
or to give a helping hand when it was wanted."

The Servants' Home mentioned above is in
Bessborough Gardens, and is supported by a lady
who was an intimate friend of Annie's, for the
especial object of befriending young workhouse girls.
The first time Annie undertook the duties of the
place was in the year 1875, and during that year
she remained seven months in the Home. The work
was, in many respects, well suited to her, and she
performed it admirably. It came naturally to her to
occupy herself with the interests of others; it cost
her no effort to remember exactly the sort of situation
that the young nursery girls, or the kitchen maids, or
the poor little "generals" might wish to obtain. Her
sympathy with them all was unfailing, she was full
of pity for the hardness of their lives, and bore their
burdens upon her heart in a wonderful way. For her
own ease she was somewhat too anxious about them,
too fearful of making the least mistake and of bringing
trouble upon any girl by inexpertness on her part in
the selection of a place for her. She would lie awake
at night pondering over the affairs of the young
servants, and planning their lives. When the more
serious business of the day was over, she used to give
easy instruction to the girls in the work-room, or
read aloud, or play games with them. On Saturday
afternoons it was her great pleasure to take the

younger ones into her own little sitting-room, and give them all a lesson in some sort of needlework, telling them stories meanwhile, or encouraging them to talk to her about their homes—their fathers and mothers and costermonger uncles, who promised that they should never want for a "happle or a pear."

If she got some desponding thoughts from the histories of the children, she found plenty of food for her sense of humour in the confidences of the mistresses. The mistresses confided in her quite as much as the children did : one day it would be the scandalised mistress whose maid had presumed to remove the "centre-piece" from the drawing-room table who claimed her sympathy; another time she would have to condole with the lady whose "general" was unfailingly to be found, drabbled with soap-suds, attempting to wash the kitchen floor whilst her grate was full of dust and dead cinders, within half an hour of dinner-time, and whose husband was that kind of man that he *could not* be kept waiting for his dinner, but was obliged always to have it "just so."

Kathleen O'Meara (Grace Ramsay), in a portrait which she drew of Annie after her death in the *Catholic World*, thus speaks of her during the time she passed in this Home :—

" Her love for each girl was peculiar and unfailing ; her sympathy was ever ready; her hope even for the most hopeless amongst her charges was Christ-like in its power, giving strength to the faltering, guiding the double-minded into straighter paths, drawing out

the best in all. Her belief in goodness seemed almost
to create it in those whom she so perseveringly tried
to help.".

The same writer says :—

"And it was not to the poor only that Annie Keary
gave her sympathy. It was especially drawn out
towards young writers, many of whom sought counsel
and help from her in the beginning of a literary
career. From no one of these did she turn away
uninterested ; often finding some little service that
she could render, and never failing to speak a word
of encouragement to the traveller on that up-hill
road which she had often found difficult to climb in
her own early years. She had that rare and gracious
gift of discerning the ore amongst the dross; and
where many a less sympathising counsellor would
have found nothing to praise, she was able to draw
one or another good point forward into the light, and
show the young beginner how to do the best that
was in him."

When the time of her charge in Bessborough
Gardens came to an end, Annie went again to the
south of France, and with her sister and a young
friend spent the following winter and spring in the
same little country home at Pégomas where she
had stayed four years before. Her descriptions of
the place in the letters she wrote to her friends,
show the loving care with which she studied
its natural beauties, and the pleasure she found
in them. There had been times in Annie's life
when she had not been able to meet the outward

joy of nature with that quick response which makes
harmony with it; when its glory and abundance had
seemed to her almost like a senseless mockery of
human want and pain; but feelings such as these
were hushed then in the peace of God which filled
her heart. "Oh! Lamb of God that taketh away the
sins of the world, grant us Thy peace," was the
ejaculatory prayer that rose to her lips whenever
anything especially beautiful pleased her in our
walks under the olives and in the valleys. The
delicacy of no flower escaped her, she used to spend
hours in studying the flowers, and would sometimes
say that she could scarcely wish for greater happiness
than in learning the delicate forms and colours that
made each one so beautiful. "I could spend a long
life contentedly here," she used to say, "with you,
amongst the flowers." One day, after she had been
making a careful painting of the lovely wild pink
gladiolus that grows amongst the corn at Pégomas,
she said, "I have been thinking how much goes to
the making of that one little flower—how important
each curve of every leaf is, how necessary every shade
of colour to its perfection; and I see in it a symbol of
the making of a soul, of the need that there is for
the unfolding of each natural beauty and for the
ripening of every grace; it may compel infinite
labour, it may take millions of years to make one
soul perfect—the mills of the gods grind slowly—but
the work, we may be sure, will have no flaw in it
when the time is complete."

Annie makes us see the scenery of Pégomas, in

her novel of *A Doubting Heart*, as her heroine, Emmie West, saw it.

" Emmie remained for a moment, shading her eyes with her hand, to refresh herself with as much sunshine as possible. . . . Madame's Valley, with all its scattered dwellings, lies spread out like a panorama at her feet. The groups of houses she spies from her high station, here, by a red roof in a bosquet of grey olives, there, by a thin volume of smoke rising through the thick, high canes that border the river ; these all contain friends and have associations for Emmie now. She knows who owns that group of fig-trees, whose branches hold up buds like delicate green cups, high in the air ; whose is the orchard of quince and almond at the opening of the valley; and to whom belongs the vineyard on the other side of the winding road, where the dwarf vines have clothed themselves promisingly with downy leaves and clusters of a good smell. Ah, the winter is over and done indeed ! . . . .

"Emmie ran down the steep steps into the flower-garden, then swiftly down the garden path between rows of sweetly smelling beans, till she reached the point where the hill dipped steeply towards the ravine, and there she stood still to listen. The cicalas and the green frogs were making a little less noise than usual. Above their harsh voices, and above the tinkle of the distant rivulet, Emmie distinguished three clear liquid notes coming from an almond-tree half way down the near side of the hill. Ah ! and now three other notes, liquid, sweet,

answer from beyond the river. Again the call and
the loving sweet reply. Emmie had never heard a
nightingale's voice in her life, but she does not
doubt their identity to-day, for Madelon had told
her that nightingales would sing all day and all
night in the valley when spring had really come.
She smiled to think how many quotations would
have risen to Mildie's lips on such an occasion.
'Most musical, most melancholy.' Oh ! no, not
melancholy at all. English nightingales might be
melancholy singing at night in solemn cathedral
closes, but that one in the almond-tree on the hill,
singing in the hot, hot sunshine, with a cloudless sky
overhead and countless flowers below, was so happy,
and had so much to say to his love in the orange
grove on the opposite slope, that he did not know
how to hurry out his notes fast enough. Emmie
would not disturb the sweet talk by walking through
the coppice, so she turned up the hill and determined
to take another and longer ronte to the Orange-tree
house, where she had promised Madelon to call that
afternoon. . . .

"By the time she reached the path leading down
into Madelon's valley, she had lost sight of the
village and gained a wider horizon. More and
more valleys, more and more olive-crowned hills;
farther and farther away patches of party-coloured
fields, showing like fairy gardens in the golden afternoon light ; and farthest of all, between the opening
heights on the far horizon, another blue, deeper
more dazzling than the blue overhead, a moving

living radiance, the blue of the Mediterranean, melting and losing itself in the trembling sky-line.

"It was almost a rest to turn into the green darkness of the pine-wood after looking at so much light, and Emmie made her way quickly to the head of the valley, where a tiny mountain rivulet burst from the rocky hill-side and began its course through the ravine. A flock of sheep and goats conducted by a young shepherdess followed her down the steep; and for years afterwards whenever Emmie thought of La Roquette, it was that particular scene and its accompanying sounds and sensations that came vividly back to her. The tinkling of the sheep bells, the gurgle of the rivulet, the rough ferns and mosses that choked its shallow bed, the little shepherdess's shrill voice calling her dog; deep evening stillness but for those sounds, and a sense of solitude greater even than had been felt on the lonely road with its wide views. Here there was only the dark vista of the pine-wood she had passed through, the sheltering hill-sides all around her, the depths of shadowy verdure at her feet, and, above all, a flowing line of crimson light where the height from whence she had descended caught the rays of the setting sun. Her heart echoed back the peace, the joyful calm, with which the little valley, from its crowning crimson height to its cool emerald depths, overflowed. All within her was in harmony with the outside serenity."

It was with Annie just as she describes it to have been with Emmie West in the story. She knew who owned each group of fig-trees, and to whom every vineyard on the terraced slopes belonged, whose red roofs showed in the bosquets of grey olives; and almost all the dwellers in the houses and the owners of the fields were intimate friends of hers; she made herself acquainted with all that concerned them. The Madelon of the *Doubting Heart* is a portrait of a real little Marie of the real La Roquette who told Annie her true love-story under the orange-trees.

Writing to a sister-in-law, Annie gives a slight picture of the sort of life she led in her southern home :—

"I have so much to tell you that I hesitate to begin. I know I cannot do justice to this place, or give you any idea of the odd kind of life we live here, under several sheets. The one drawback to it is that we are so much out of the world that the cares of housekeeping take up more time than is convenient. We have only got a little peasant girl out of the village to cook for us, and she has no notion of cooking according to our English ways. I really have to cook every single thing we eat. . . .

"We have made a great many friends in the village, which is at the foot of the hill on which our house stands, and in some of the scattered farmhouses in the little valleys all about. There is a lovely valley at the back of our house, which we always call 'the Orange-tree Valley,' because in its centre there is a group of houses with orange and lemon trees in front. The inhabitants of these houses are very great friends of ours—we made

N

acquaintance with them the last time we were here ; and now whenever we walk through this valley— which is our most beautiful walk—we are sure to be waylaid and obliged to come into one house or another to take refreshment, consisting generally of a peculiar sort of wine, very thick and sweet, manufactured for home consumption by the people here, raisins dried and steeped in oil, also of home manufacture, sourish home-made bread, sometimes a delicious slice of melon. All the houses of this group belong to four families, brothers and sisters and cousins of each other, and as they have very few children between them, a great part of the valley will eventually belong to a very pretty girl, called Marie Mül (*Marie du Vallon*), of whom we have seen a great deal. She is the great *partie* of the village, and has a private little romance of her own touching a poor young man who has been drawn for a soldier, but who is to return to the village this spring, in time, I hope, for the third volume of her novel to be enacted before our eyes. She has confided in us all through the winter, and promises to bring Stanislas (that is the hero's name) to see us as soon as he comes back. Of course this private choosing is greatly out of rule in a French family, but Marie excuses herself by explaining that she and Stanislas when boy and girl of ten went up together for their first communion—a circumstance which is considered to constitute a strong tie of friendship here. Ever since, they have loved each other, Marie says. Marie's father and mother are indulgent, and will

most likely give in.   Don't you think this romantic
story will have to come into a novel, with all the
lovely Pégomas scenery and the odd ways of the
people for a background ?   I don't know that I shall
have time for it, but won't you come here next
winter and work it out ?   How I wish you and Anne
could see the flowers here ; what a treat it would be
to see you paint them.   I have been trying to paint
a little.   Do you remember a time in the dear old
Addison Road when we did some studies of pots and
pans together ?   The pots and pans of this country
are perfectly enchanting.   I don't know what you
would feel if you were to see the *cruche* in which my
hot water comes up every morning ; but I think if
it popped into your room instead of mine by chance,
you would jump out of bed for your paint-box and
make a picture of it on the spot.

"We have been having some bad weather lately—
rain, and one fall of snow.   We set off after dinner
to-day in a gleam of fine weather to get a little air
and warm ourselves, but the rain came on and swept
out all the hills before we had got many yards on the
Grasse Road.   We met two forlorn little children,
and with some difficulty made out that they had set
off to walk to Grasse —five miles—up the mountain ;
their mother had gone there earlier in the day to
buy potatoes and bread, and, tired, I suppose, of
being alone in the house (they live in a lonely little
cabin on our hill-side), the two little things had set
off to find her.   We persuaded them to come back
with us to the *château,* as they call this cottage, and

now they are very happy in the kitchen, chattering *patois* to our little servant, after having had a good meal, wound up with the French children's luxury, confiture and bread. We gave a children's party on New Year's Day—but I must not begin to tell you about it at the end of my letter, but keep the story of the Pégomas children's attempt to play English games and eat plum-pudding till another time. I must now thank you for all the kind, sympathising things you say about *Castle Daly*, and congratulate you on your own work. I am just now writing my Christmas story for the *Monthly Packet*, on the proverb 'Noblesse Oblige.'"

The following is part of a letter, also written from Pégomas, to a young girl in a house of business in America, who had formerly attended some classes at a night school in Kensington—the Aubrey Institute, where Annie had been in the habit of teaching. Annie was very much attached to this girl, Emma, and corresponded regularly with her :—

"DEAREST EMMA,

"I am afraid it will seem long to you before you receive an answer to your dear letter, but it was made a longer journey than even you expected it to make. It has followed us to the south of France, where we are spending the winter. You know we had left Bedford Gardens before I wrote last, and were taking charge of a Servants' Home. We stayed there seven months, and had a good deal of hard, but very interesting, work there. Last

November we came to France. A great friend of mine has a little farm for olives and vines near Cannes, and on the farm there is a pretty little *châlet*, which she has lent us for the winter. I wish I could make you see what a lovely place it is in which I am sitting writing to you. The window is wide open, and I look down (for our house stands on the side of a hill) on to a plain all laid out in olives and gardens; on each side of it are beautiful mountains, some dotted all over with olive-trees, but the higher ones are clothed thickly with dark pines, and the highest and most distant are bare and purple. Between the furthest hills we have a glimpse of the Mediterranean. This is our front view. Behind the house it is still more lovely. We overlook exquisite green valleys, with orange gardens and plantations of fig, and quince, and peach, and almond trees; then corn, and vines, and olives on the slopes of the hill, rising higher and higher to bare grey rocks, and above these the snow range of mountains, looking oh! so dazzlingly pure and white against the dark blue sky. We have had lovely weather nearly all the winter; we shall go home with a fresh stock of health, and with all sorts of lovely and happy pictures in our minds, to be a store of joy that we may rejoice in even when we are too old to go out and see anything fresh. I wish I could hand on some of this pleasure and peace to you, it would do you so much good in your hard life. Don't you think it is a help to know that there are beautiful, peaceful places on the earth? One sees

in them what God is, and catches a glimpse of
the kind of joy He means us all to have one day.
You can't think how sorry we are for all the sadness
and all the trouble your letter tells us of; but, do
you know, it does not altogether make me sad for
you. The thought it chiefly brought to me was,
'Oh! how precious the soul of that dear child is in
her heavenly Father's sight, that He lets it be tried
in such a fire, that it may be brought to the perfection He means it to have,'—moulded and graven,
as the most exquisite silver and gold images have to
be moulded and graven, through heat and by blows,
till it is wrought into the beautiful and perfect like-
ness it is meant to wear. You are a beloved child of
God, a sister of Christ, and there is an eternal life
of happiness and glory before you; don't mind if you
can't feel it or even think it now, it is true all the
same. I know that our dear Lord is just teaching
you and leading you by the hand, and that your
doubts will end in peace. Won't you take this as
a message from Him to you through me? I prayed
that He would tell me what to say to you, and
this message of love is what He sends. You will
see the truth about the eternal life soon; I don't
think it is possible to live up to the highest point of
duty *and of happiness* without this. I know one can
go on doing one's duty thoroughly under clouds of
doubt, and even in complete unbelief; there are
many who do, and they are dear to God, but the
duty is done sadly or deadly, without the spring of
life and joy that we are meant to have. That

fountain of life and strength is hid in God. Christ showed us the way to it, and we get it into our souls when we utterly trust Him and give up our hearts, and our lives, and our aspirations to Him as to a faithful Creator, who will not leave unsatisfied any of the longings of the souls He has made; who will not let love die, or disappoint finally the cravings for joy, for perfection, for light and knowledge that He has implanted, and that are parts of Himself, immortal as He is. You say, How am I to be sure? When I get back to England I will send you some books that I hope may help you to be satisfied of it in your reason—there is reason enough.

"It is a great comfort to have our reasons convinced, and study and thought will help to that; but I believe the great thing to be sought is a direct word of God to the heart, not to the reason. He can show us His light, and feed our hearts with His strength and love. . . . . He feels for you in all your grief for your mother, and she too yearns over you still with deeper and holier yearnings than any she ever felt in her earth-life; but there is no pain in them now, for she sees the end, and knows that the darkness and suffering are only for a little while— that it is through this loneliness and darkness you are being prepared for eternal joy, and love, and bright companionship."

To a girl whom she had known in Bessborough Gardens, an invalid, she wrote :—

"My dear Mary Ann,

"We are very glad to have news of you, and
to hear that you are getting through the winter
tolerably well; I wish we could send you some of the
delicious soft air and the glorious sunshine we are
having here. Sometimes when I am looking at all
the beautiful things about us, the mountains with
their pure white snow-peaks, and the hills crowned
with olives and vines, and then down into the green
valleys enamelled with flowers of all colours, I feel
as if it were a foretaste of heaven, and I should be
almost sorry to have so much to enjoy without
sharing it with all whom I love in England, if I did
not know that all this is but a glimpse, a faint show,
of the glory, and the joy, and the beauty, which is
reserved for us all by and by. No words but words
from the Psalms can express the exaltation one feels
in seeing such beautiful works of God as are all
round us. 'O Lord, our Governor, how excellent
are Thy ways in all the earth,'—one keeps saying
sentences like these as one walks along. I wish
I could show you the way we went this morning.
We set off directly after breakfast, and first climbed
up a steep road which winds between two valleys,
with a view of purple and snowy mountains in the
distance. The sky was much bluer than it ever is in
England, and when we looked back, we saw the sea
showing like a purple lake between the mountains.
When we had gone some distance, we turned into a
side road which led us into a beautiful pine-wood, so

fresh and dark and shady; we followed a narrow wandering path that took us first to a little place in the hills, from which a bubbling stream bursts out, then down into a lonely, sloping olive grove, which made us pause and stand silent for some time, to think of Mount Olivet and of what happened there. You cannot think what beautiful things olive-trees are, and how full of light and sunshine they are, seen from above, and yet what a solemn peaceful shade there is below when one gets among them. The olive grove we were in to-day made us so well understand why an olive garden should be a favourite resort of our Saviour's, for it seemed a place made for prayer. This one was on a hill-side too, so we could really think it like that one.

"From our olive grove we went on and on, always down by little winding paths, and at almost every step we came upon some lovely flower, purple and white violets in hundreds, anemones, white narcissus, aconites, rare kinds of ferns. I send you a little nosegay of them, to give you a faint idea what it was like. At last we came to a group of houses standing at the bottom of this lovely valley. The people who inhabit these houses are well off and happy on the whole, but some trial comes into every lot, and amongst them there is one poor invalid whom we had come to see. She has something the matter with her chest, and she coughs as badly as you do in spite of the sunshine, which indeed she does not much profit by, for she hardly ever gets out. She was very much obliged to us for a pot of English

preserve, but what she cares for most is for people
to come in and talk a bit to break the dulness of
the day. She cannot read, and has no books, and
no one to read to her. The little room she lives in
is such a curious dark place, with a wooden shutter
instead of a window, and an open fireplace; over it
there hung a pot with all sorts of strange herbs in
it, from which she was making a medicine for her
cough. From her house we went to another little
place, where an old man, also an invalid, sits nearly
all day in a dark shed making baskets; and then a
girl called Marie Mül came out, and begged us to
come in and rest a little in her mother's house. She
took us up to a cheerful upper room, where she had
been sewing. Oh! dear Mary Ann, I should like
to show you that upper room, and for you to sit and
sew there sometimes with Marie Mül. The window
was open, and looked out into a group of orange and
lemon trees, on which the sun was shining so
beautifully that the fruit looked really as if it were
made of gold. Just by putting out your hand, you
could gather as many ripe oranges as you wanted.
And such a delicious scent of violets came in at the
window. Marie is very happy, I think, sitting working there, but there is one thing you would not like
in her lot, she never reads, has no books, and had
never even had a Testament till we gave her one.
They have a great many things in their valley that
we have not, but they want the pleasure of reading,
which you and I think more of, perhaps, than any
other that comes into our lives. We would not

change our books for oranges, or even flowers and sunshine, would we ?

" As we were going home, we found a very curious insect called the praying mantis. It has a face like a wizened old man's face with a night-cap on his head, and it has two things just like hands in front, which it holds up and clasps as if it were praying. The people here whenever they see one, call out, ' Pray thou for me, good little fellow.' . . .

" I hope I shall soon hear again a good account of your health. . . .

" Your affectionate friend,
" A Keary."

Annie's old friend of school-days, Lizzie M., had died a short time before this second visit was paid to Pégomas. She writes from there to Lizzie's only child, a dear young friend of hers, whom she always called her niece :—

" Darling Katie,

" I don't like to realise that we have been nearly a month here and have not written to you. I hope you have not been thinking that your aunt was forgetting you. We are now settled in our little home. It was very strange at first, plunging into the extreme quiet of this life, after the bustle we had lived in at Bessborough Gardens. You remember how hard it was to get a room to be quiet in there, between the girls and the visitors, and now we have this house all to our four selves,

Eliza, Clara, our little maid, and myself; and the advent of a visitor is such a rare event that it throws our little Marie into ecstasies, and it is necessary for her to find an excuse for going down into the village immediately, to tell her friends all about it. She is such an odd contrast to our Bessborough Gardens' maidens, our stray Mary Annes and Marthas—so much better mannered in some ways, and yet on the whole more confidential and familiar. She will come into our sitting-room any time in the day that she finds herself dull in the kitchen, and enter on some long story; she thinks nothing of coming behind us to see if the books we are reading have any pictures in them. . . .

"By dint of watching us and asking questions, she has learned to do a great many things, and she can't bear us to do what she has learnt to do. She delights in setting out the table very elaborately for tea. She puts everything she can lay her hands on upon it; once she served up a little sauce of pepper-corns and allspice as a new delicacy. She is so pretty and picturesque-looking in her homespun coarse striped petticoat, and bright coloured shawl crossed over her shoulders, and gold earrings and high-heeled shoes, her head on one side, as she stands looking at us out of her pretty brown eyes. . . .

"They have a very pretty custom here of each child, when she makes her first communion, choosing a friend to go up with her, and then the two girls remain close friends, communion friends, through life. So we find that if we make acquaintance with a girl one day and ask her to the *château*, she is pretty sure to bring her communion friend with her; and in this way our acquaintance spreads quickly. As I was coming over the bridge just now, from our kitchen to the house (for the kitchen of the *châlet* is a separate building, connected with the house by a sort of bridge), I saw two of the communion friends sitting up above in the hayloft; they called out to me to wish me good evening. They had each got an orange, and they were eating and chatting side by side in the hay, as happy and loving as two pigeons. They are quite inseparable, one is hardly ever to be seen without the other.

"You know how much I am thinking of you, and wishing to be with you at this time of the year. I shall be with you in thought and prayer on Christmas day, at the holy feast. You know that your precious mother was my communion friend. I love so to think that this tie is closer now than ever, that we can all meet together at these holy happy times."

In another letter to Katie, she says: " The orange trees are in flower now. Marie Mül has promised us some branches from the tree near her window; when they come we are going to pack them up with some roses and send them to you. Perhaps you may be able, to lay them with a greeting from us on the dear, dear grave. I do so think of *her* when I see all these lovely flowers, and when I am trying to paint them. Nothing brings her back so much to me as looking at lovely things, such as I know she is

among now. You and I must be a great deal together in future, and I must tell you all the sweetness and goodness that your mother showed me in
the early days when we were so much to each other.
Every little word I can recollect about her I will
treasure up for you, for everything about her
is so precious, and is an inheritance that belongs
to you. In my life her loss makes such a dreadful
blank. . . .

"I wish you could have been with me at church
at Cannes on Easter Sunday. The church was *so*
lovely with palm branches and roses, and we had, I
think, the most beautiful sermon I ever heard
preached on an Easter Day. The text was, 'Till the
day dawns and the shadows flee away.' It was all
about the joy of resurrection, and the strength that
the certainty of that joy ought to give us while we
are still dwelling among the shadows. Separation
from those who have passed before us into the full
daylight was spoken of as one of the shadows, and I
wish I could give you the sweet, brave words in
which the preacher encouraged the bereaved ones to
bear it, bidding them *dwell* on the joy of meeting
again, and cherish all the tender thoughts and
remembrances that would make the meeting not like
a fresh beginning, but just a taking up of the love-
life where it had paused for a little while. The
shadow was only on our side, he said, we were to
remember there was no break, no want on the other.
They were living in union with us, even when we
could not feel it. Then he went on to say how every

trouble was only a shadow that the dawn would dispel, and that we should find an answer to all our doubts and troubles in remembering constantly that death was in no sense an end, and that this life was only as it were a school, in which we were being prepared for what was to follow, when all our ideals would be realised, and all our loves perfected, and our yearnings after happiness and goodness receive the fullest satisfaction.

" I don't know who the preacher was; he looked as if he had known a great deal about the shadows and was getting near to the dawn."

On her return to England Annie devoted herself to the writing of her novel, *A Doubting Heart*, the greater part of which was written at Brighton, where she spent the winter of 1876-77.

She was happier whilst engaged upon this book than she had been in her work on any previous one, for she had begun to feel greater confidence in her vocation, on account of the kindness with which *Castle Daly* had been received.

She writes to a young friend, whose acquaintance she had made in the south, whose mind and character interested her very much, and whose literary sympathy she greatly valued :—

" I have had an industrious summer, and am enjoying my story more than is usual with me. I think it must be all the kind things said about *Castle Daly*, and the pleasant knowledge of old and new friends being interested about my work, that

cheers me on. I have got my four heroines well
advanced in their histories, and I hope they will
interest other people as much as they do me just
now; though really I ought not to expect that; it is
like a mother hoping that strangers will care about
her children as much as she does. The child of my
four I like best.is called Christabel; she is a dreamer,
and something of a genius. I find it very interesting to try to show how the inside world of her
dream shrouds her from the outside world, till the
shock of a great love comes, shattering unrealities,
and leaving her bare of experience to meet the new
power that has come into her life. I am sadly afraid,
however, that I have not skill enough to show other
people all or half of what I mean."

"I am getting on fairly with my book," she wrote
to one of her nephews about the same time. "I
have now thought out a long way ahead of my
writing, and *if* I can only write it as I see it, I think
I shall be far better satisfied with this book than
with anything I have written yet. But there is a
long way between seeing and writing; it is like
looking over an unconquered country that has to
be won inch by inch."

Annie was not so much taken up with her work
during these winter months as to be forgetful of the
concerns or the interests of her friends. Some of
her most characteristic letters were written at this
time to several of them; and they show how much
her thoughts and her feelings concerned themselves
with the lives of others.

To the friend mentioned above she writes in January, 1877 :—

"I want to wish you a very happy New Year. I wonder how you feel about New Year's wishes. I am sorry to say that I remember a time when I used not to like them, and when they made me sad and despondent instead of hopeful. I know that it was because I was in a wrong state of mind : too much set upon one way of being happy. I now see how happy I have been, though I have not had the life I wanted ; and my wish for all I love, particularly for the young, who are looking forward to their lives, would be, first of all, that they might begin with the knowledge I am ending with—that all things work together for good to all, though it is only when they love God that they can see the working. . . . .

"I was really enjoying my writing more than I had ever done before ; but just now there has come rather an uphill time. Shall I tell you about it ? Yes, I think I will ; for it is not fair, since your thoughts are turning in the direction of authorship yourself, to show you only the pleasures of it. Well, there are times of great discouragement, when one feels almost to hate one's self for living in a world of shadows, while one's dearest friends, are living through actual heart agonies. One knows one can do no good by turning heart-sick from one's own task, that it is cowardly and weak to do so, and that one's duty is, as Macaulay says, ' to go on writing doggedly'; but the difficulty of getting really interested in the shadows is all the same. Actual life looks so real,.

O

and its reflection so dim, when anything has happened to awake a very vivid feeling. As I have begun to write a melancholy letter, I will tell you a piece of news that has helped to sadden us. Do you remember that Pégomas girl, Marie Mül, who showed us the linen she had spun and the stockings she had prepared for her trousseau? I told you, I think, that she had confided her love-story to us, and that it was a very pretty one. Marie reckoned securely upon her lover coming back exactly what he had been when he left the village, and was perfectly happy, showing a very simple confident sort of affection, which struck us as promising a great deal of happiness in her tranquil, sheltered life. Well, we have heard from her, and she tells us that her lover has just married another woman, a person a great deal older than herself, whom every one knows that he does not love. I suppose she has money, but Marie does not say so. The Marie in my story tells her love-tale to my heroine in a chapter called 'Red Anemones.' I feel quite ashamed of the discrepancy between fact and the ideal of it now; but I suppose it would be very miserable if fiction did not give the beautiful side of life."

In a letter to the same friend, on the subject of writing, she says:—

"I think nothing good comes easily,—often facility in composition only proves that the thoughts are commonplace, or there is no struggle to find expression for them, or a facility of composition may come from the faculty of imitation, which enables beginners to catch other people's styles, and serves very well for a time, but is really a hindrance in the end, as it interferes with the formation of a natural style of the writer's own. If there are thoughts worth giving from one mind to another, I think there will also be somewhere, for them, the outside form of words which only can properly fit them, and which ought not to be adopted, but drawn out of the writer's soul if the mind-children are to be complete, not aliens. I think it is best when the thoughts come first and clamour for expression (like souls seeking bodies) till they find it. There is a great deal of pain about it as about all births. We don't all grow up alike or evenly; sometimes the shaping power lags far behind the thinking and feeling part of the creative faculty."

To the same young friend, who had been telling her of a literary scheme of her own, she writes:—

" I am not surprised to hear that you have a feeling of discouragement; that was only to be expected, and what I believe no first book was ever written without its writer experiencing scores and scores of times. But I am grieved that you should have worked so hard as to be really ill. It does not really matter how slowly a book grows; I am sure that the best books have been built slowly, and I can tell you for your comfort that I have often found when I have been stopped in the middle of a book, and had to wait doing nothing at it, perhaps for months, and not even thinking of it, that it had grown with gigantic strides in the dark, as it were in my mind, and that I could write it twice as quickly and as well, when I turned to it again. I had two long breaks in *Castle Daly*, and I am very glad of both now as I look back, for I am sure I wrote better for the enforced resting times. I consider that you have got your story quite formed enough in your mind for it to grow by itself, without your troubling about it when you can't work. The plan of it will be like the piece of thread that is let down into a cauldron of boiling sugar to make sugar candy. The crystals will form round it while the liquid is still, and when it is looked at all the beautiful shapes will be seen to have arranged themselves ready for use. So your thoughts will gather and take shape round the thread of your story while you are not even thinking about it ; so the waiting time instead of being a hindrance, will, I venture to predict, be a time of growth and enrichment—only have faith to wait. . . .

" Have you ever noticed the motto Mrs. Gaskell chose for the title-page of *Mary Barton*—a motto from Carlyle—look at it. It is my chief consolation to remember it whenever I begin a book, and I mentally affix it to every title-page I write out, though I cannot adopt it, as Mrs. Gaskell has made it hers. . . .

" No, I do not want you to make your story end miserably, you had better not ; but you must not fix it to one life. The use and the charm of writing is that it helps one to help others to get *outside* one's own experience. Writers can do this better than their readers, it is a real escape into a life one fashions for one's self for a time, and if one does not let it hinder one from action in the actual, I think it is a healthy escape from the imperfect present, to the ideally perfect future. I know I have not said quite what I mean."

To the same :—

"I cannot help feeling sure that your impulse to write must come sooner or later, and that it will bring a great joy to you. There is *so* much pleasure in expression—pleasure that outweighs all the struggle. I do not think your thoughts will let you rest till you have begun to make word clothes for them. I have drifted into saying this to-night because we (that is, my nephew Charlie and myself) have been sitting by our window this rainy afternoon looking out on a melancholy little leafless windy Brighton Square garden, and have been thoroughly enjoying a long talk about the pleasures and pains of writing, and the right way to seize and make permanent the impressions and suggestions that crowd upon one at times (oftenest when least expected, on dreary outside days like this) in vague fleeting forms that are scarcely recognisable from an emotion, till one tries in some way or other to make them speak.

"I am very glad to hear that you are so enjoying your English winter, and that you have got such good work to do in teaching in the school. I do not think anything is really more satisfactory than the sort of work a person like you can do among girls of a different class—drawing out the real refinement and womanliness that is so often kept down by

circumstances in rougher life. There is so much
more in every one than they know how to bring
out, and the sort of help a cultivated person can
give to one less advanced is like helping to set a
soul free.   If it is only giving them greater power of
expression, making the meanings of a greater number
of words clear to them, it is opening the way for the
soul to grow. Then if one does chance upon a
starving intellect to which the scraps of knowledge
one can give are real food and drink, how delightful
it is, and what touching love and gratitude is sometimes drawn out in this way.   Such a happy chance
came to us once in a pupil we had in a night-school
in London.   Of all the young girls I have ever had
to do with in the way of teaching, rich or poor, she
was the one who loved learning most, and was most
thirsty for every bit of knowledge she could get
She used at last to come to me alone, she got so far
beyond her class, and read Milton and a book on
optics which delighted her beyond anything.   It was
so pleasant to read the delight in her face when a
new thought came to her, or when she began to take
in some description or comparison in the poetry that
had been dark to her at first, from her having lived
all her life among the sort of things which gave her
no recollections to compare it with.   She has gone to
America since, and the letters she writes to us are
still full of gratitude for that little bit of teaching ;
it makes me quite ashamed.   I believe if it only gets
to the right people, there is no gift in the world that
wins such love as the gift of culture which a lady

can give to a girl who has a nature that wants it, and circumstances that hinder her getting it."

To the same she wrote in answer to some questions of speculation upon religious subjects :—

"May I tell you what I think is the real danger of reading books of doubtful theology, and that is, if you read them *before* you have sufficiently studied the evidences in favour of your own belief, to feel that you are standing on sure ground, and that you can judge whether the writers have arrived at their negation after due search and fair reasoning, or if they have merely taken up the negative side from foregone conclusions because it suited the condition of their minds, or because they had been shocked at some aspects of popular teaching and chose to consider them bound up in the teaching of the Bible, without searching the Bible for themselves to see if this is so. What gives one pain and disturbs one's mind in reading sceptical books is the tone of certainty which the writers take in speaking of the articles of faith they have rejected, as if the facts on which these rest really had been disproved, and could no longer be held by fair minds. The best way to cure this pain is to go into the questions of evidence for one's self as far as one can. You will then see how *very* unfair the assumption of certainty is, and that the people who assume it, often without meaning to be unfair, have not arrived at this certainty from study of evidence, but from some metaphysical or scientific assumption, which to their minds appears more certain than any evidence, as, for example, that no miracle ought to be believed, or that revelation from God to man is an impossibility. To me it has always been the greatest help to turn back to the facts as history shows them, and to try to get a firm hold on the reasons for and against their having actually taken place. Westcott's *Canon of Scripture* is a book that helped me much. One gets so puzzled by the tone taken by sceptical writers with respect to the gospels, as if their authority had been almost disproved, that it is a comfort to go back and find how very strong the evidence in favour of all the canonical books being genuine really is.

"Perhaps all this is not at all what you want, and the questions that fascinate you may be of a much more spiritual and metaphysical kind. I only suggest, in case in pursuit of thought on the more inward sort of spiritual problems you should suddenly find that you had not made your foundation sufficiently sure, and should tumble into a sea of perplexity that a little previous study might have saved you from."

To the same :—

"I want very much to have a talk about H. Martineau's Life with you. I have not had it yet, but years ago I read her letters to Mr. Atkinson, and I think I understand the sort of painful impression her life must have made on you. She was a wonderful, noble woman, and I can't tell you how I admire a great deal of her writing. She was a sort of ideal to me, and for years it was my most cherished castle in the air to get to know her; but I have felt

more and more through her later writings that there
was something about her sort of imagination that
made her no rule for other people—something
abnormal in her character which caused her on some
subjects to take a distorted view. I think it was
this peculiar sort of imagination which accounts for
her being able to be happy after giving up all belief,
and that therefore it was more an intellectual than
a moral defect. No, I am wrong ; the defect in her
was neither intellectual, nor moral, it was spiritual.
The imagination somehow concerned itself only with
the intellectual and the moral, and left the spiritual
in everything out. Do not you feel that in her imaginative writings there is no spiritual imagination, and
that her people are all more or less qualities or
opinions ? I am sure you will not struggle out of
your spiritual difficulties on that same barren side,
I should be sorry if I feared that for a moment.
H. Martineau could be happy while all the spiritual
side of her slept ; but what a loss it was ! How great
she would have been if she had been developed all
round ; and now that she knows the truth, how sorry
she must be that she missed the chance of teaching
it here. Do you remember what Maurice says about
'being ashamed at *His* appearing ' ? About really
good and noble people who had not accepted Christ
on earth, when they saw Him and found that it *was*
He who had been inspiring them, and loving and
guiding them, and giving them the eternal life they
had come into without expecting—how they would
be ashamed of their want of love and trust, and feel

as a child feels who has distrusted a parent who has been working for it, and loving it all the time. So sorry to have lost the chance of *trusting* while they did not *know*.

"Do you know, I can sympathise with what you say about want of liberality. It is very difficult to combine fervour, a real strong grasp of what you believe with perfect liberality to doubters. It is only the *strongest* faith that can do that, such faith as Macdonald or Maurice have—the faith of people who having had a vision of God themselves, and being as sure of Him and of His mercy (nay, a thousand times surer than of their own existence), can leave those who appear to be working against Him, with the utmost serenity, to His leading, not even dreading the harm they may do others."

To the same :—

"I do not know why you should wish you were not interested in theology. What *is* there more interesting, or worthy of a soul made for God, than the study of how to know Him? As for the puzzles, what else can we expect? Would it be God that could be found out easily, by a few of His creatures' faculties in a short life-time? We have all eternity to learn God in; it would be a poor prospect if we could get very far into our lesson here. We must expect to be puzzled and baffled again and again, only do not let us get impatient and weary of the search, or feel tempted to think that He is nowhere because we cannot yet reach to the height of His vision. We are perhaps not using *all* our faculties in the effort to see. You say the great question is, how far we are to give our reason free play? I think we cannot give it too free play, but we must not trust to it alone, or use it in the wrong way, that is, I think, in speculation instead of in looking at facts. We can't reason without some premises to reason on. We must know something about God before we can reason on His nature or doings. Reason does not, I think, in this search come first. God must speak to us Himself; we must look for Him in our own hearts in answer to our prayers; we must wait, and wait, and hope, and trust till He draws the veil and gives us a glimpse of His countenance, then let us speak of what we have seen. I believe that inward road is the best road to God. Whilst we are waiting to see Him ourselves, let us listen to those who do see, and trace what the knowledge of God has done in other souls. It may not always be knowledge that we shall find, but it will be love and moral height, and there, as in a mirror, we shall see God. Do not you think that after all it is only the heart of God that we can expect or need want to see much of here? It is so manifest that we can never in this state know much of His ultimate purposes or designs, except that they must be in accordance with His heart—must be loving. Then about teaching others; it is the heart-love we want to give them, the certainty that love is at the centre of the universe, and that our business here is to subdue all in ourselves to love."

To the same :—

"I am glad you did not change your mind about sending me that dear letter, for indeed you do not know how much I like to hear your real thoughts and how deeply interesting they are to me, nor how ardently I wish I had light enough to be a helper to you. Never mind, however, God is His own interpreter, and He is only waiting his own time—the right time—to show you Himself, and to fill your hungry and thirsty soul with a satisfying knowledge. What I should like to say lovingly to you is to go on as you are doing now, teaching your Sunday class, and going to the Holy Communion, and continuing your usual services, and prayers, and readings, waiting patiently for the good in them that *will* come. I know how hard it is, I lived very long under such a cloud myself, but I am so very glad now that I never let quite go my hold on the outward ordinances, for I think I might never have come to understand them, as I do now, if they had ever grown unfamiliar. I think while you are going on attending to them for the sake of others, the light of God's face will dawn upon you through them, and bring you full certainty and peace. I do not believe that a satisfying knowledge of God often comes to the soul by soundings of the intellect. It is right to search, and try and satisfy the reason—and it can be satisfied —and give a glad, complete consent to all that inward illumination brings; but I think it is only a dry, outward kind of knowledge of God that can be proved. The Spirit must speak to the spirit before *that* knowledge of God which is life, and joy, and power, can come to us. And God speaks in His own time. We are not always ready for that light. Perhaps there are times when the soul may need a certain twilight and doubtfulness for its growth, just as we put hyacinth bulbs into the dark for their roots to grow downwards before we let them feel the sunshine, and begin to stretch up their stems and blooms to the sun. You know what feeble flowers a hyacinth bulb has when it is brought to the light too soon, before it has struck down long fibres into the water. May it not be that the souls which are meant to flower most gloriously towards God, have to grope about a long time in doubt and uncertainty? Would it not be a pity for them to turn despairing and leave off growing roots of patience and hope, and self-knowledge, to conclude that there is no light because they have not been lifted up into it? I hope I am not saying anything that will sound to you arrogant. It is not arrogant in my meaning, because I am so sure that God is teaching and leading even when we seem to be unsuccessful in our search after Him. Joyful certainty of His inward presence and His personal love is only another stage of His teaching, a further showing of the gift that is given when the soul first sends out a cry of longing after something higher than itself. I am glad you feel that to have a high view of the manhood of Christ one must believe in His Divinity. To me, all hope for the human race lies in my belief in the fact that the Divine became human, and has made it possible for us, for *all* humanity, to share His Divinity. How shall I ever be able to tell you what I think and feel about this, in letters? To me it is just the key-note of everything, and sums up all philosophy and all hope. I don't feel as if I could understand anything on any other supposition, neither God, nor man, nor nature, nor history. It would all be chaos if I did not believe in the last grand act of creation—the adoption of our human nature into the divine. It explains development, it explains all past mythologies and revelations, and the yearning of all nations after God, as, so it seems to me, nothing else could explain them. But, in a short space, how can I give you my reasons for saying this? I cannot go beyond assertions, and to state one's own standpoint is not by any means to justify one's having got there. May I tell you a few books to read that will show you the road by which some people at least have come to a belief in the divinity of Christ after a great deal of trouble? Have you ever read any of Coleridge's *Aids to Reflection?* If you do not know anything of Coleridge, and find a plunge into him rather formidable, I wish you would get Professor Shairp's *Essays on Poetry and Philosophy*, and see there what he says of Coleridge, and of the phases of mind through which he passed. Shairp has written two more books that I want you to read. One on *Religion and Culture*, and one on the *Aspects of Nature*. Do get *Religion and Culture*, I know that you will like it, and that it will help you. Have you ever read any of Hinton's books? *Man and His Dwelling Place* I think you would like ; and may I send you a little book, now out of print, called *God and the Sacraments?* It is written by Mr. Farquhar, a mystic, and is full of most wonderful teaching. I think it says more helpful things about the real meaning of Communion than any other book I ever came across."

Writing to a cousin about some books she had been interested in, she concludes :—

"Have you read the *Symposium in the Nineteenth Century?* Don't you always feel as if you should like to put an oar in, for that everybody goes wide of the mark, and that the arguments on *all* sides are left unanswered, more or less ? I suppose no one can really on these subjects put into words the thought down at the bottom which convinces him, and is the real root of his opinion. The *roots* of our convictions lie so deep, and belong so entirely to the nature of our souls, that I suspect we never can really *explain* them in words to each other. We think so and so because that is the only mould for thought we have within us, and we can't turn out anything in a different shape."

To her young friend in America she wrote several times during this winter and spring :—

"DEAREST EMMA,

"I am afraid you have had a very sad time and that your faith and patience have been sorely tried. It is our faith and patience that are precious to God. I believe that if we could only see before-hand what it is that our Heavenly Father means us

to be—the *soul* beauty and perfection and glory, the
glorious and lovely spiritual body that this soul is to
dwell in through all eternity—if we could have a
glimpse of *this*, we should not grudge all the trouble
and pains He is taking with us now to bring us up
to that ideal which is His thought of us. We know
that it is God's way to work slowly, so we must not
be surprised if He takes a great many years of
discipline to turn a mortal being into an immortal
glorious angel. When you write again tell me still
more about yourself; I am so glad that you have
found some friends among Mrs. Pearsall-Smith's
friends. I have often prayed that you might, and I
do thank God for having put it into your heart to
persevere in going to the meetings, and for having
raised up this friend to you. If you ever have a
chance of seeing Mrs. Pearsall-Smith herself, do take
advantage of it, and if you speak to her, give her a
message of love from me. Say it is from a grateful
heart, whom her words in England helped to trust
God a little better than before. . . .

"I know you will like to know a little of what we
are doing this winter. . . .

"We keep up our connection with the girls we
knew in Bessborough Gardens, and often have such
touching letters from them—this, you can imagine,
increases our correspondence. I am also writing
again, and as I feel that I want my books to be
letters to those I love, to make up for the scantiness
of my real letters, I am having sent to you two books
of mine that have been written since you left

England. One is called *Castle Daly.* I was writing
it that winter when you used to come to us in
Bedford Gardens, and we had such nice French
readings together; the other I have written since.
It is a children's book called *A York and a Lancaster
Rose.* I hope you will accept them both, as a visit
from me, and that you may find some thoughts in
them that may make you feel as if we were talking
together again. I wish they were worth more, and
that I had the power of writing more from my inmost heart, and that it were given to me to bring
out higher teaching. I find I can only speak a word
here and a word there, and I do not aspire to much
more than amusing people, and giving them a rest,
after perhaps some difficult bit of work or hard part
of life. To do this for people like yourself, dearest
Emma, is a great joy to me, and I hope you may find
these books useful in soothing away some tired
evening. Do you get Mr. Macdonald's books in
America? I have just been reading one called
Thomas Wingfold, which I like better than any
other of his I have ever seen. There are such
beautiful, beautiful words in it about God's love to
all, and about the sunshine that a knowledge of Him
can make in the soul, even when outward circumstances are dark. And besides these words to the
heart, there is a great deal of help to puzzled heads,
a great deal to clear away doubts and difficulties such
as one cannot help hearing about in this age of the
world."

P

To the same :—

"MY DEAREST EMMA,

"Here is the first Sunday after the Epiphany, and I have still to wish you a Happy New Year.

"I am at the Servants' Home in Bessborough Gardens now, taking charge for a fortnight, whilst the Lady Superintendent is away, and a very busy time I am having. I am so sorry for some of the girls here now; one is a poor, forlorn, sad-looking girl of nineteen, no father or mother, brought up in the workhouse, and unlucky in having got a very hard place the first time she went out; she was absolutely ill-used, and became very ill. She says she has never slept in a comfortable bed in her life before she came here; think of that, and she is nineteen, and she has seldom since she left the workhouse school had enough to eat. She looks starved in every way, body, soul, and mind; I am so sorry for her. . . .

"Thank you for writing such a nice letter and for loving us so much. Oh! you are very much mistaken if you think it is not a great joy to us to be so much loved by you. What is there so beautiful as love, and such love as we have for each other is the most beautiful kind, because it is founded on real sympathy, and tends I trust to draw us both nearer God who is Love. How can you, with your loving heart, say you do not know God. Do not you know that 'Every one that loveth is born of God and knoweth God,' for love is of God. Jesus says that the second commandment to love the neighbour is *like* the first, to love God. All that is good, and high, and pure in our neighbour, is of God; and in loving that we love God, and all that is bad in our neighbour we must pity and forgive in the spirit of God, and in so loving and pitying and helping, we experience the love of God in ourselves and learn God. Yet there *is* something more, a yet more individual way of knowing and loving God, and I expect that is what you are yearning for. I do not think myself, it is so important as the other way of loving God which is *like* the love of the neighbour. This individual love of God, as a personal friend and guide and helper, only comes through a habit of prayer, and the experience of help and guidance one gets from bringing everything to Him, and asking for His light upon it. It is a great blessing and gift, and like nearly all other great blessings and gifts cannot be had without seeking. Can we know a friend if we never go to see him, and never take the trouble to talk to him, and listen for his answer?

"'Ah!' you say, 'but how am I to listen?'

"Answer to God's saying, 'Seek ye my face,' 'Thy face, Lord, will I seek;' and see if He does not show you His face and let you hear His voice. I cannot tell you how or where, for He has a different way of speaking to each of His children. Perhaps it will be down in the depths of your own soul, by the opening out of a new joy and peace, that you will find Him; perhaps the knowledge will come in a new sense of His nearness in the beauties of nature; you will see His love and His mind written all over the spring skies, and lettered in spring flowers about the earth. Remember that every beautiful *thing*, and far more, every beautiful soul, is a thought of God; by which He reveals Himself to you; the most perfect revelation having been made in the beloved Son, who came to show His glory in a life of lowly deeds of love and self-sacrifice. Cannot you admire and love that sort of glory? Is it not really what your soul loves and would fain be? . . . . I am so glad at what you say about the Church services; I love to think each Sunday that we have joined in the same prayers, and read the same Epistle and Gospel and Lessons. Is not the Epistle beautiful for to-day (2nd Sunday after Epiphany), and don't you like to think that Christ showed forth the Father's creative power and glory first in such a *kind* act as saving some poor simple people from being shamed and hurt in their hospitality by having no wine to give their guests?"

To one of the little servant-girls whom she had known in Bessborough Gardens she wrote:—

"My dear little Katie,

"I was very glad indeed to get a letter from you, and to hear that you are well and happy. I hope you are trying hard to do all your duties. I am glad to hear that you sew so much, for you know you had a good deal to learn in that way. I hope you will get to be a real good needlewoman, and that you will take a great pleasure in your needle. I am

very fond of sewing myself, and I think there is *so*
much pleasure in learning to do anything with one's
fingers really well and beautifully. Do you remember
my showing you the beautiful way in which the little
wild flowers I brought home one day were made ?—all
the little leaves finished off with such delicate fringes
of soft hairs, and the blossoms so carefully fastened
on to the stalks, and the seed vessels fitted so neatly ;
and we said it was a lesson in finishing off work well
which God gives us in every little flower and leaf.
He never leaves anything half done; not the tiniest
little moss or weed has an end or an edge that is not
most beautifully ornamented and finished off. It
is the same with shells, even with rocks and stones.
God makes everything perfect to its last little atom, to
show us how carefully we should work. We should
not be satisfied with the things we make looking well
in a rough, outside way; we should find pleasure in
turning out work that will bear looking at all
through, as His work will. I have been staying at
Bessborough Gardens. There are two little girls
there now who did just the same work that you used
to do. Their names are Nellie and Rosie, and they
are very nice children. They used to have lessons
with me in the afternoons ; and on Saturday afternoon I let them have a treat of guessing riddles
while they mended their stockings, as you used to
do when you were with us. I am sending you some
of the riddles I told them. I have put the answers in
the corner, folded over. Are you getting too old for
riddles, dear Katie ? I think of you always as ' my

little woman,' as I used to call you; but you are
getting quite grown-up now. Do you ever get any
flowers where you are, I wonder? Some day, when
spring has quite come, I will send you a little box of
flowers, that you may see again how beautifully they
are made, and take another lesson about the way in
which we must do our work to please God.

"Your affectionate friend,

"A. KEARY."

To a young girl in a Reformatory, whom she had
known as a servant-girl, she wrote :—

"We have got some pretty hyacinths out in our
room just now; I wish you could see them. I will
tell you a little thing that happened to one of them,
because it seems to me a sort of parable. It is a
white hyacinth, and one day when all the little buds
were on the stalk folded tight together, ready to
unfold in the sun, the hyacinth-glass was put upon
the window-ledge that it might get more light. A
little while after I came into the room, and, not seeing the flower, I opened the window, and, in doing
so, knocked the top of the hyacinth against the
blind, and broke off five or six of its buds, and
bruised the green leaves. We were so sorry, you
cannot think. We said, 'Here is our dear hyacinth
quite spoilt ; it will never be worth anything now,
all one side of the stalk will be bare and ugly, and
there will be scarcely any flowers at all. It is hardly
worth while to give it fresh water, or put it in
the sun. However,' we said, 'it will perhaps turn

out better than we think, so we will go on putting it
in the sun and see what will happen.' Shall I
tell you what has happened? It is the best of all
our hyacinths now. The kind loving light healed
the bruised leaves, and drew one of them close to the
stalk, so as quite to hide the bare part under a green
veil; then the buds that were left, having plenty
of room to grow, got larger and larger, and curled
round the stalk and spread into beautiful, large
white bells, the fairest and sweetest of all our
flowers now. Do you want me to explain the meaning of the hyacinth's history to you? No; I think
you have read already the lesson God has been teaching us in that flower. Is it not that love, which is
like sunlight, can heal sin and sorrow? and that
people who have sinned and suffered may become
even better, stronger, more beautiful in their souls,
than if they had not suffered or done wrong? that is
to say, if, like the hyacinth, they turn to God's love
and light and let it heal them. I will send you one
of our hyacinth bells to keep in your prayer-book,
and put you in mind of its story."

To a young friend, on the subject of judging
others, she writes :—

"Do you not see that nearly all anger comes from
misunderstanding? If we could get inside any one,
our greatest enemy, the person who disgusts and
wounds us most, we should get revelations that
would surprise us, and that would melt all our dislike into tenderest pity and love. Pray for God's
light in which to see others, and then you will be at

peace, for you will love. The great thing to help against irritation is always to try to get out of your own point of view into other people's, and find out how things look to them, then you will always be able to make excuses for them."

To a young girl, who had just left school, she wrote :—

"I think this is such an important year of your life, and such a difficult year : the getting into regular employment when you have to plan for yourself. I used always to be getting more to do than I could manage; there is great fret and worry in always running after work, it is not good intellectually or spiritually. I wish I could help you; but I am so often in this state myself that I hardly know how. I think I find most help in trying to look on all interruptions and hindrances to work that one has planned out for one's self as discipline, trials sent by God to help one against getting selfish over one's work. Then one can feel that perhaps one's true work—one's work for God—consists in doing some trifling, haphazard thing that has been thrown into one's day. It is not waste of time, as one is tempted to think, it is the most important part of the work of the day—the part one can best offer to God. After such a hindrance, do not rush after the planned work, trust that the time to finish it well will be given some time, and keep a quiet heart about it."

In the year 1877, after two winters spent at a distance from her friends, Annie returned to London, and made a home there, at Campden Hill Gardens, in the home of the two nephews with whose lives her own had been so closely interwoven. She seemed to be floating in a sunny sea towards a safe and pleasant harbour at the end of her life ; the doubts and struggles were over, and she was reaping the fruit of conscientious seeking and of careful work. In *A Doubting Heart* she makes Mrs. Urquhart talk of having reached the last stage of her life's journey, the state which Bunyan describes in the *Pilgrim's Progress* under the name of the Land of Beulah, " where sweet breaths from the heavenly hills blow tranquillity and peace about the heart." Annie felt as if she had reached her Land of Beulah, when the greatest happiness of her life seemed about to renew itself. She would have been content to remain a long time there, with a heart at leisure from itself, and thoughts occupied with the future of the younger generation, waiting for the summons to go over and possess the larger life—if such a lot had been in store for her.

From the new home she wrote to her young friend in America on the 14th October, 1877 :—

" This is a lovely day. I think St. Luke's little summer has begun, and I hope you will enjoy your longer and more beautiful fall-summer where you are. I was thinking this morning when we were walking up and down Notting Hill Square, looking at the half-stripped trees in the garden, where the leaves are quite brown and sere, or, at best, a dull yellow, of what you told me about the exquisite crimson and gold of your American trees in autumn.

I do hope that you will enjoy them this year, and they will give you some beautiful, hopeful thoughts.   We have just been getting some little rhododendron trees for our balconies, which are to flower next spring, and I do so like looking at the already fully formed buds, next year's flowers, getting ready now, showing through the old leaves that will fall off before their beauty begins.   The leaves have nursed the future flowers all the year, and they will die when the flowers are ready to bloom, just as our bodies fall off and die when our souls are ready to flower in the spiritual world.   One sees this clearly with the rhododendron buds, because they are large in autumn, but I believe every single leaf has a bud in its charge which it shelters all the summer, and then it dies to give its nursling air and space to grow in.   The law of sacrifice and of hope is read to us, you see, by every autumn leaf that the wind blows in our faces, whether they are brown, or, like yours, crimson and gold.   Yes! but I like the crimson and gold ones best, they are like contented, happy old people, who understand that the end is better and more glorious every way than the beginning—just a going on from better to better.

     "This has been the harvest festival at our church; we thought of you, and I gave thanks for your love as one of the precious things that I have to be thankful for.   I wondered whether you were rejoicing in a sweet autumn Sunday. . . .

     " I have got a thought for you that I will tell you here.   Swedenborg says, that in the spiritual world love constitutes nearness, and hate distance. A spirit, he says, must always be near what it loves. Love draws love to itself in the spiritual world by the same sort of attraction as matter draws matter here. So we may say there is no space with God, because He loves all, and so is near to all. Those who do not love Him, however, put Him far from them, for you know, spiritually, hate and dislike make distance. In proportion as we love much we partake of the nature of God, and get rid of space ourselves. Our bodies do not hold us if we are loving, for we are always sending out our souls to our friends and loved ones. A selfish, unloving person is shut up in a little space—in self—and is so much nearer to being an animal, so much further from the nature of God."

Before the buds of the rhododendron she speaks about in this letter flowered,—"the already fully-formed buds, next year's flowers, getting ready now," —the whole aspect of the future was changed for Annie.

A little anxiety about her health had been growing up all the winter, so slight that it scarcely seemed to forewarn danger; but, unknown to herself, or to any one else, she was the victim of a disease from which recovery is very rare, and which had been secretly sapping her strength for some time. Only a little cloud on the horizon, and in one day the whole heaven was overcast.

PART V

ANNIE went out quite cheerfully on the morning of
the 2nd of March, 1878, with her sister and her friend
Emelia, to take advice upon the symptom that had
roused the indistinct fear mentioned above ; before she
turned to go home again her friend knew that she had
only one year more to live ; Annie knew too that a
sentence of death had been passed upon her. All her
life she had dreaded more than anything else what was
unexpected : it was more difficult to her than it is to
many people to turn the gaze quite away from one
aspect of the future to another. She was just then
so happy too ; she counted up all her treasures, those
that she had won, all that had been given her, whilst
other conditions of being, untried paths, loomed
pale and ghostlike on before. Relations and friends
had already passed on there, it is true, but she was
clinging with fonder affection than ever to those who
remained, and in the harmony to which her nature
had attained was giving out in greater abundance

than before the divine spirit of joy and love. Her
pale face showed the anguish that she felt, but she
did not complain, she only prayed for help to lay
down her life contentedly at the call of God, and the
help was not denied to her for which she asked; if
there was mortal suffering, there was as certainly
divine peace. She told Emelia afterwards that the
first words which came into her mind upon awaking the morning after her visit to the physicians
were, "Accepted in the Beloved," and it is quite
true to say that the comfort those words brought
with them never left her through all the suffering
she had subsequently to bear, nor during all the
fluctuations of hope and fear she passed through in
the year that lay between that morning and the
morning of her death. Within a few days after she
heard the opinions of the doctors she prepared to
undergo an unusually painful operation—the only one
possible in her case—that she might give herself the
chance of a prolonged life, it seemed as if there were
a possibility of reprieve for some years, and she
clung to the hope of this. Emelia, who was with her
during the whole of the long day of suffering on
which the operation took place, wrote of it to a
friend : "It is wonderful how she has been supported
through her sufferings. Her look of calm and perfect
peace I shall never forget, and there is not the
slightest effort or exaltation. It was just as if it
were the most natural thing in the world to lie still
in a Father's arms."

Shortly after the operation, which appeared to have

been fairly successful, she wrote to one of her friends :—

" I must send you a line in pencil of warm love and thanks for your sympathy. I feel to-day as if a new wave of strength had come, as if I had come to a turning-point, and the currents were setting towards life again. Dear, will you pray for me, that this experience may not be lost to me, but that the life given back, if please God it is given back, may be more instinct with the true life than the previous years. I long to tell you a little about this experience. It was such a sudden being brought face to face with death. I ought to learn a great deal from it, and I have been wonderfully shown the tender Fatherly love that appointed every step of the way. You know too, don't you, dear, that it is worth while to suffer to learn Him ? . . .

" The first proof of my new book came just when I was most ill, and now I am able to enjoy correcting it."

To her little Katie, also, she wrote about the same time :—

" You cannot think how pleased I was to get your letter. I am writing to you in pencil because I am not yet strong enough to sit at a table and write with ink, but I am getting much better. It has pleased God to restore me after a very serious illness. Dear Katie, you too last year were very near death, and I think you must know how solemn it is to feel that God has given one's life back to one. How careful we must be to use the years to come altogether in our blessed Saviour's service. To have had a very serious illness, and to be brought back from it, is like a second gift of life, and should make us feel doubly that we owe all our time and all ourselves, ·body, and soul, and spirit, to God. I shall not be able to write you a long letter to-day, but I am sending you the little writing-case I promised you a long time ago."

One of the greatest trials of Annie's illness to her was her being obliged to leave the home in which she had only spent a few months, instead of the years to which she had looked forward. It was considered necessary that she should be removed to Eastbourne, both for the sake of the sea air there, and for the opportunity the place offered of her being put under specially skilful medical treatment. No place could be quite like a home to her away from her family and friends. Yet she always tried to feel contented and restful wherever she was forced to be. Several changes had to be made from one part of Eastbourne to another, during the changes of the seasons as they came round. On the first evening of settling in a tiny cottage close to the sea, she said, looking round upon the little room, made pleasant to her already by the presence of a row of books upon the sideboard, "What a little place contents us! How much I shall enjoy the quiet here!"

" We have just moved to a tiny little cottage," she wrote to a friend, " close to the sea; it is quite a nut-shell, but so pleasant, and the view we have from

our sitting-room window is a continual feast. . . .
Our end of the parade is the old-fashioned end, so
we have the advantage of being quiet and free from
bands. I really think I am getting stronger, and
mending week by week, though the progress seems
slow, and the pain very lingering, and apt to return
with the least fatigue."

Her love of nature seemed to be as great and
almost as joyful as it had ever been. The colours
of the sunset upon the shore, the moonlight ways
across the water, the launching of some little pleasure
boat at evening, the trailing of the fisherman's net
along the sand, as she watched them from the window
of the little cottage during quiet hours after days of
pain, brought just the same contented smile to her
face, and the same whispered prayer to her lips, as
the sunlight, and the flowers, and the rich colours of
the south had been wont to do in her days of hope
and pleasure. She was very fond of those evening
sights upon the shore, and used to lean forward in
her chair watching them for long times together.
The window commanded a view of Hastings, and
she liked to see the lights of the town spring up in
the twilight, when the colours had faded from the
nearer part of the picture. She seemed very happy,
looking and admiring—a little dreamy, too. Perhaps
it was not only the things she saw with her outward
eyes that soothed her and made her smile.

Writing to the friend of her Egyptian travel, with
whom she had corresponded for so many years, she
says :—

"I confess I am rather disheartened to find that my doctor wishes me to remain here longer. I thought I should have been at home, or perhaps for a little while with you again, before this. It seems a long banishment. . . .

"We have just heard of Ellen T——'s death from her sisters. It was so beautiful and peaceful. Just at the last it was given her to feel the joy of the life on which she was entering, so vividly, that the pain of parting with her husband and little children, terrible as that had been in prospect, was, when the time came, quite swallowed up. Her sister wrote that on leaving her death-bed she could feel nothing for a few hours but a triumphant sense that it was life, the true life, on which she had entered. . . .

"I wish I could show you the view from our window just now; the sea is like glass, the sky a soft tender grey, with all sorts of wonderful pearly lights in it reflected in the sea; and two or three little boats are in sight, one with a bright red sail glowing so beautifully on the cold sea and against the grey sky. In the foreground we have a strip of tawny-coloured beach, with three Martello towers in sight, lessening in the distance, and a stretch of distant coast, purple and dark grey to-day. You would make a lovely sketch of it. Before I end I must say how glad I am that you are reading Richter's *Flower*, *Fruit, and Thorn Pieces*. There are some parts of that book I am so fond of. Have you noticed a piece about the 'Last Day of Spring,' and the 'Dream of the Dead Christ'?"

The following letters written from Eastbourne to two of her young girl-friends (adopted nieces, not nieces by relationship), show that personal suffering had not deadened her powers of sympathy with the sorrows or the joys of others :—

"My darling child," she writes to the daughter of her old friend Lizzie M——, "how I wish I could see you; but, alas! I am still being kept on here. I can only tell you by letter how I long to comfort you. How much I should like to have you here, that you might put your dear golden head upon my shoulder and talk out all the troubles and puzzles. I might not be able to help you much, but you would feel how I love you, and I could at least assure you from experience that all these morning clouds that hang about your life just now will pass away, and that sunshine and peace will come. Do not for one moment think that either your Father in heaven, or your precious mother, is in the least degree vexed with you for your doubts or your troubles of mind, whatever form they may take. They feel nothing but the tenderest sympathy and the most utter love; and, what is more, you must receive the troubles, yes! even the perplexities and doubts, as tokens of love. God is leading you up through them to a higher stand-point, educating you to know Him better and trust Him in a more thorough way by and by. Only, do not let go your hold on prayer. Have no reserves with God; ask Him with confidence to lead you every step of the way. Then do not be anxious, for all will come right. Wonderful things are wrought by prayer. It is the hand stretched out into the region of miracle which brings the power of God, and the help of God, about us. He is always longing to help, but prayer is the means by which the help comes. And you must *carry* your cross, not let it drag on the ground. I am thinking of a little picture in a French book. There are two figures, each with crosses of the same size, climbing a hill; one figure has taken his cross on his shoulders and is marching bravely and lightly on, his head lifted up to the blue sky overhead, and scarcely seeming to know that he has a cross to carry at all. The other figure is letting his cross drag behind him, pulling it up after him with, oh! such tugs and strains over each little stone on the road, always obliged to look behind him, never able to take his eye off the cross for a moment, and feeling its burden and its hindrance at every step. The motto to that picture is, '*Il ne faut pas trainer ses croix.*'

"You will take yours up bravely, looking upward and thinking of your mother, who carried her cross in her youth, and, I am sure, knows what you feel. I think she is telling me to bid you take courage now. . . .

"Do not grudge if you have to give a great deal for a little to your fellows; for God is an ocean of love, and is ready to give Himself to you."

The following is to another adopted niece, the Clara who was her companion at Pégomas during her second visit there:—

"MY DEAREST NIECE,

"Alas this is our address still, and I see no immediate prospect of being allowed to go back to our dear home. I should so much like to see you. Your bright happy letter has done us good, like a sunbeam on a dark day. It is very pleasant to hear of all the happiness that has come to you, and of the delightful holiday you are having. . . .

"I must tell you a little about ourselves. I have not been so well lately, I have been suffering a great deal of pain. I am obliged to keep very quiet, and am hardly allowed to do anything; a short letter now and then to a very dear niece or nephew is the limit of my tether. It is so odd to lead such an idle life, and to look back to the dear, active days at Pégomas, when you and I did all the cooking together. Shall I ever make a pudding or a pie again? Oh, how nice it would feel to be strong enough to do it—to have two free hands again! I often blame myself now for not having been all my life thankful enough for health and strength. These by themselves are great gifts to be thankful for; yet when they are taken away, God gives us other tokens of His love and His nearness, and thus turns our losses into gains. I have had so many things to make my illness sweet, so much love and kindness shown to me, that I should indeed be ungrateful if I complained."

To a very dear old friend, the young teacher whom she had loved so much in her childhood, Annie wrote from Eastbourne during one of her suffering times :—

" What you tell me of all your dear ones interests me so much. Dear little Tattie ! I can see her just as she was when we met her in Geneva—a young edition of yourself—and I can imagine her now exactly like that bright, sweet friend when she used to let us have conversation days. I fancy her with just that dear light on the face, and the little red smiling mouth, and eyes full of humour and sweetness. How I should like to hear all about your children . . . .

" I am grieved to think of your suffering. Ah! I know what the suffering of ill-health is now as I never understood it before, and you have known the trial so long, and struggled under it so bravely. I think that you will find there is a lovely crown of joy for you in your next state. Will you let me come and see you in the heavenly house you will have ? Shall we talk over old times there, and will you show me this treasure and that ? Each one will be the outcome of some one of your struggles and labours, or of some painful, tearful day on earth. I do not mean in the way of reward. Still our Lord unites the sufferings of His people with His own, and I cannot but think that every pang borne with Him in our earth-life will be found to have borne some lovely fruit when we get into the land of realities, and see the end of all the discipline. I must not write any more. I am glad to hear you have a nice early service ; I cannot get to early services now, but

I manage to go every Sunday to the Holy Communion."

Annie was too weak to remain through the whole of the morning prayer, so she used to go to church about the time when that was nearly over, and wait in the porch in her chair listening to the closing hymns of the service until the Celebration began. She said sometimes that she felt being there listening to the voices and the music inside the church was like getting close to the door of heaven.

When Annie was first taken ill, or rather, when she first knew of the danger that lay before her, some parts of her novel, *A Doubting Heart*, still remained to be written, and all that was written needed revision. She was much disturbed at first, thinking that she might never be able to make her book complete, and she had always felt great remorse at the thought of time wasted, or of anything left unfinished. To find a way out of the trouble, she applied to her friend Mrs. Macquoid, whom she asked kindly to promise that if she should never be able to do anything more at her work, she would take it up just as it then was, and finish it for her. "The great favour I had to ask of you," she wrote, "was nothing less than that if I did not live to write the three last chapters of my book, you would write them for me, so that all should not be quite wasted. You do not know what a consolation it has been to me during this illness to th nk that I could ask this favour of you, and to reflect on your goodness which made me think that you would grant it. You will understand better than perhaps any of my other friends how much I wish I had *quite* finished my story before all this happened, but if, please God, I do live to write the last chapters, they ought to be better—ought they not?—for what I have experienced."

Annie was able to attend to her writing again during the year that succeeded the operation, but when she died there was still a task left for the friend to perform without which the work would have been incomplete. Mrs. Macquoid used to write to her each month as the parts of her story came out in *Macmillan's Magazine,* kind letters of comment, which showed with what care she was following the development of the characters and the plot; she was anxious to get into the spirit of the book so as to be able to carry out Annie's intentions faithfully if the necessity for her help should arise.

These letters were a great comfort to Annie, and the discriminating tenderness that was shown in them touched her with the deepest gratitude.

It interested her to read her story month by month, and she cared very much to finish it in the best possible way.

"I want to know," she wrote to a friend, "how you like the last two numbers of *A Doubting Heart.* I hope you like Katherine Moore. I am getting near the end now, but it is slow work. I cannot dictate, as some people can, straight out of my head. I have to scribble it all out in pencil first in the

rough, so it is a double process, and I am never able
to go on long at anything now."

To her nephew she writes :—

"I am leading an almost entirely idle life here,
though Wynyard is actually in the middle of reading
the fateful letters that have been shut up so long in
the cork drawer, and Madame de Florimel, who has
left him to read them in the orange-tree valley, is
waiting dinner for him at the château. I have pro-
gressed so far, and got to the most exciting part of
the story, but I am leaving it almost untouched,
and am sacrificing my mornings to sitting out on the
beach; generally listening, and with pleasure, to a
bad band. . . ."

Through all her suffering time Annie was very much
like what her father had been in his, exceptionally
patient and cheerful, and grateful for the least service
done, careful for the rest of the nurses, never seeming
to think that pain or weakness made the least excuse
for selfishness or impatience, or that any one else's
comfort ought to be put aside for hers on account of
what she was suffering; she was like her father, too,
in being able to enjoy her usual pursuits and pleasures
to the last. The writer in the *Day of Rest*, who draws
a picture of Annie in her little London home, adds
another picture, as she remembers her at this time. "It
rises in my mind as distinctly as the first," she says,
" but is painted in purer, tenderer colours. The brightness has faded, but there is a holy calm and sweetness
about it which more than compensates for the loss.
This is as I last saw Miss Keary during her long,

painful illness, when she sat on the shore at Eastbourne, day after day, reaching it with increasingly
feeble steps, till as she grew weaker, even the sea
breeze, which had revived her at first, exhausted her
failing powers. I see her with the same calm expression and interested smile upon her face, finding
constant pleasure in the changing colour of the sea,
in the close inspection of a flower, or a shell, never
losing her graciousness of manner however she might
be suffering, always grateful for the most trifling
services of those around her."

As long as she could get out upon the beach, or
drive along the roads and downs, she carried on her
habit of shell and flower collecting almost with her
old zest. She was quite eager to find her favourite
shells, and used to make up little collections of them
to send to some of the young servant-girls she had
known at the Servants' Home, and with whom she
still corresponded.

To Katie she writes :—

"I am afraid it is a long time since I wrote to
you, but as you will see by my writing, I am still
an invalid, and writing is one of the things that tries
me most, and brings on the pain from which I suffer.
I can think of you, however, dear little Katie, and
pray for you, when I cannot write to you, and I do
think of you a great deal. I am sending you by this
post a little box of shells that I picked up for you on
the shore here in the summer. One day when I was
feeling stronger than usual, I got down on to the
sands, and I found a good many shells, and I thought

of you as I picked them up.   I thought, ' These sunny
blue waves have washed these shells ˙to my feet for
Katie.   They are a message of God's love to her, and
they will tell her the same story about Him that the
flowers told her; she will see how lovely and com_
plete all God's smallest works are, even those that
are hidden in the depths of the sea, and it will
encourage her to think that God's eye of love is over
all His works, that He wants them all perfect, that
He wants *her* to be quite good and loving and true
in her soul, and to do her work in her degree, whatever it is, as carefully and beautifully and with as
nice a finish as He does His.'   Look, dear, at the
lovely marks and colours of these shells, and at the
beautiful little hinges which bind the pairs together ;
each shell is a lovely little house made by God for
some tiny sea-creature to live in. . . .

   " I send two pairs to you to show you how they fit
together ; and now I must say good-bye, dear Katie.
I am better on the whole, but not nearly well yet—I
do not think I shall ever again be as strong and well
as I used to be, but, thank God, I suffer less pain."

   When Annie could no longer walk about to
gather shells or flowers herself, but could yet spend
a little time out of doors resting, she used to talk
to her attendant in a way that made the time of
service full of amusement to her, giving her short
lessons, in botany it might be, one day, or at another
time drawing a story out of her endless treasure-
house of tales.

   "I have been reading a paper in the *Cornhill* on

the origin of flowers," she wrote to a friend. "Reading it seems to open to me a wonderful glimpse into the loving, educating character of God's providences. If flowers and insects through such long processes are brought to suit and beautify each other, and to bring out ever new powers and joys for each other, does it not give us a wonderful hope of what may be going on in ourselves? How we are being educated for new glories and powers? The little germs, the longings that we feel in ourselves, are to meet their development in conditions necessary to draw them out into fulness and satisfaction, somewhere, some time, in the length of eternity. I cannot half express what I mean, but read the paper in last May's *Cornhill*, and it will bring the thought to you, though the writer of the article speaks as if the flowers and the insects adapted themselves to each other, and there were no loving intelligence guiding the processes to their perfect end."

When there were no outdoor pleasures left to Annie of any kind, and she had grown too weak for change, reduced to just the invalid's round between bed, and couch, and chair, from sunny window place to warm fireside corner, her love of reading remained as strong as ever; a book was always able to soothe her in pain, or amuse her in weariness, as long as she had strength to prop one up before her, or power to concentrate her sight upon the printed words. All sorts of books interested her; she almost wondered at herself for being so much absorbed in so many different subjects. Books on

science, history, light literature, all had their turns
with her; she used to fear sometimes that she could
not be very spiritually minded, as she was not able
to confine herself to the reading of religious books.
It comforted her to remember that it had been just
the same with her father all through his illness, that
he had read as discursively as she did, and that up
to the last month of his life the most important
moment of time for him was that in which he
inspected the supply of books from Mudie's that was
to last him for a week.   He and Annie were more
afraid of being left without a book, than of any
other small misfortune that could befall them.

Writing to one of her nephews, she says :—

"The books you got for me were all right, and I
think will prove sufficient for the month.   The only
drawback to the volumes of *Fraser* and the *Cornhill*
is, that they are too heavy for my lame hand, and I
can only read them when I can prop them on a
table.   I have been reading a most touching Saga
written by a modern Icelander.   It is a sort of
journal kept by an Icelandic farmer, in English, and
given to a traveller by his widow, who publishes it
in *Fraser*.   I call it touching, because the poor man
was an intense lover of books, and had taught himself English in order to profit by the stray volumes
he could pick up from English visitors to Iceland.

" Such entries as these occur.

" ' Saw Mr. ——, who kindly gave me an *Illustrated
London News,*' or ' a number of *Household Words,*'
or ' Mr. —— has promised to bring me a handsome

book next spring.' The handsome book, I am afraid, proved to be the *Adventures of Mr. Ledbury*, by Albert Smith. The account of the monotonous life and the long winters, and the occasional feastings and quarrellings at weddings, remind one very much of the old Sagas. You must read this when we are at home together."

And again—

"If you should ever chance to have half an hour to spare at your club, I advise you to read a paper in the September *Cornhill*, called 'Child's Play.' As a contrast to Pater's paper, I think it is worthy of attention. I am quite charmed with it; it strikes me as beautifully written, and as showing a real understanding of an imaginative child's way of looking at things. The writer takes a different view of child life from Pater, and I think a much truer one. He considers that children are defective in sensation, that all their perceptions of outward things are far less vivid than those of a grown person, and that they live almost altogether in a world of phantasmagoria, which is much more important to them than anything outward, and which cuts them off from the grown-up people's world.

"There is a good remark at the end about the folly of expecting rigid matter-of-fact under the name of truthfulness from children. The writing strikes me as very good, quite like Charles Lamb, here and there. Of course there are as great differences between children and children, as between men and men, but yet I think there is a mental atmosphere common to all children which changes so gradually, that only a few observers (or rather a few imaginative people who have lived *vividly* the child life, and so kept a good deal of its atmosphere embedded in their memory), ever succeed in bringing it back.

"Pater is far too self-conscious, and has, I am sure, mixed his recollections with afterthoughts. I did not mean to write so much about this, but reading a paper that pleases me as much as this one has done, makes me long for a talk with you over it."

The summer and the autumn passed, and the winter drew near. Then Emelia, whose companionship had strengthened Annie during the early period of her illness, and whom the stress of personal affliction had separated from her through the succeeding months, came to Eastbourne on purpose to be with her, took a house for herself and her friends, made it as homelike as she could for the invalid, and stayed there and helped her to bear the darkening days of that saddest year. Annie had many weeks of comfort, some even of hope, in the home of the friends; she was unusually well at the beginning of the time she passed there. To a dear god-daughter she wrote from this house in October:—

"I am so much obliged to you for your dear letter; it was like a drop of water on a thirsty ground. I was just hungering to hear of you all, but wanting an excuse to write. I have had a great many ups and downs since I came to Eastbourne, and at times I felt, I confess, deeply disheartened, almost as if I ought to resign the hope of getting well, and look only towards the other exit from suffering at the end of an illness. But, dear, I do wish to stay, if it so pleases God. I am very very happy here in this world, and I love these seen things (books, &c.), to say nothing of people, so dearly, that I cling to the hope of getting better very closely, and I think now that I may do so without presumption, or setting my will against the apparent purpose of God for me. I have really made progress lately.

"We like so much to think of you at Bessborough Gardens, and we thank you with all our hearts for throwing yourself into the work so dear to us. I am very glad to see that the amusing side of it is as great a help to you as it was to us; for I do not think any one who does not get a little bit of fun out of the display of character constantly showing itself, can bear up for long against all the anxiety and hard work, without suffering. If you can laugh at the mistresses now and then, as well as cry with the poor little maids, your sympathies will right themselves and not be too much drawn upon. I am glad those two forlorn girls came to you, for I am sure you have made them very happy, and given them the remembrance of a warm sympathy to look back upon and light them over their future struggles. . . .

"Once more thank you for your sweet letter. Yes, it does help me more than you can have any idea of to think of your loving thoughts and prayers for me. You do not know how precious it is, or how it fills my heart with gratitude to God, who has given me so many sweet young ones in this generation to love and to make the world beautiful to me."

To her young friend in America she says, in the last letter she ever wrote her:—

"Though I am not any more able to write than I was, I am on the whole better. What I have to do is to be patient, and content to lead an invalid life for some time to come. I do not suffer so much as I did ; one of my chief privations is not being allowed to write as much as I like to my friends. I trust you never think I am forgetting you, or loving you less, when you do not hear from me ; and I trust you not to forget our compact to read the Epistle and Gospel each Sunday, with thoughts and prayer for each other in our hearts. I wonder whether the Epistles and Gospels have been saying such wonderful things to you lately as they have to me. I wish I could tell you how fresh and new many parts of the Bible, especially St. Paul's Epistles, have grown to me since I was ill. I see so much more meaning, and such joyful meanings, in what I thought I understood quite well before, but which now shows itself to me larger and sweeter, and more full of comfort than I found it till I needed more. There would be no use in my telling you, for God Himself will open out the meanings to you as you want them. The Bible has some special teaching for each one of us—a word of joy and tender love from God to each individual soul; and if we go on reading in faith, patiently waiting for it, that special word will find us and thrill our souls with the certainty that God Himself is speaking to us, and that He knows all our wants, and cares, and needs.

"It is only defect in us that makes it seem strange to us that God should love us and think of us every minute. If we knew more what love was, we should not be surprised; what we have got to realise is that love is at the root of life, and that the sorrow and sufferings are passing illusions that we shall wake up from by and by.

"I want to tell you about some books I have been reading since I have been ill. The ones I cared for most are three biographies of very good men—Campbell, Erskine, and Hinton. The two first lived to be very old men, and what I felt so encouraging in their lives was to trace the growing peace and almost overpowering sense of the love of God which marked their lives to the very last. The truth which was dearest to Mr. Erskine, was the universality of the love of God. He never liked it to be said that this life was a life of probation. He said that was a mistaken view of God's dealing with us, for that God was not trying us to see if we were worth anything, but educating us through all the trials of this life till we were brought into a knowledge of Him, and so saved.

"I remember telling you about Hinton's book, *The Mystery of Pain*, when we were coming home together from the College in Fitzroy Street. His theory was that self-sacrifice is the true law of life for eternity as well as for time, and that we only find it painful here

R

because of imperfection and deadness in ourselves.
When we have got rid of our mortal bodies, and our
souls are healthy and strong, we shall enter on a life
of constant service for others which will be intense
joy; it is the sickness and deadness of our souls
which makes us feel pain. He believed that all pain,
the pain of illness, the pain of over-fatigue or of
mental sorrow—all these pains, he thought—were
effecting some good, not to the sufferer, but to mankind in general; for Hinton thinks it is only through
pain and suffering that progress is made, and that
new truths and new blessings are won for the world.
We cannot see the connection now between our
sufferings and any sort of good to any one, for here
we only see such a very little bit of the whole. We
hardly know that we are part of the whole, and
consider each life as a separate thing; but in our
spirit life we shall see the meaning of every pain,
we shall see that no pang was in vain, but that all
was being used for bringing in good to the world.
I know you will like this thought, and I hope it
will help you to bear all that over-fatigue you tell
me of. It will make you happier next time you are
very tired if you can say 'This pain does not end
with me, it is to do good to some one else.' 'We
know God,' Hinton says, ' as the Redeemer of
the *world*. We are glad, not because *we* are well
off or good, but because the world is to be saved and
all men are to be made good and to acknowledge
Christ.'"

Sometimes her letters have a sadder note in them.

"You do not know," she writes to a friend in Brighton, "with what regrets we look back to those happy, happy days [the winter spent at Brighton] when we could come in to you any afternoon and have a delightful talk, and when we were nearly sure of a morning glimpse of your face. Oh ! if we could transport ourselves into such good times again. Your list of books makes me very jealous; we are very badly off as to a library here, and my last batch of books from Mudie's was unsatisfactory."

Annie used to read aloud in the evening, sometimes passages from a selection of Swedenborg's writings. She liked to dwell upon the condition of the soul after it leaves this earthly state, and upon the renewal of old dear ties in the sphere where love makes nearness, so that to think of one dear to us is to surround ourselves with the presence of the beloved.

Yet she did not speak of leaving us then, it even seemed possible that, the winter once over, there might come a renewal of strength. In reality, life was slowly ebbing away, the world was less and less with her, and the spirit shone more brightly through the gradually withdrawing veil of the flesh. It was not that any change in her likings or pursuits appeared. She read the same kind of books, and talked the same sort of intellectual cheerful talk she had been used to do, but all the time her gentleness was becoming more perfect, her patience sweeter, her love more expansive. She wished very much that she could say comforting words to other sufferers, and thought that she should perhaps write something some day that might be helpful to sick people, about her own experience, and the spiritual consolations which she had found. Any life that touched hers, in however slight a degree, interested her. She had a view from her bed, in the house where she passed the winter, of a part of the cliff where a new road was being made, and she could see a workman engaged in carrying stones from one place to another, every morning at a certain time. With a relic of the habit that she had in childhood of making up stories about people whose appearance she got to know from seeing them regularly (as she makes little Walter do in *Johnny and Nayum*) she looked for the workman daily at the appointed hour, as she lay in bed, and prayed for him that he might have a good day that day.

To an invalid sister-in-law she wrote in December :

" I hope to be better soon, and meanwhile I feel such fellowship with you in your sufferings. I feel we are one now in even a closer way than we ever could be while I did not know what it was to lead a life when the ' grasshopper is a burden,' and each little thing, getting up and going to bed and eating, involves an effort hard to make. I now do so feel for you in all you have gone through, and, as I said, we have fellowship one with another. I think of you when I am very weary; and the thought of all your sweetness and goodness, and of how you work and think of others in the midst of your pains, helps me to take courage. I want to tell you some of my times for thinking of special things, that we may be together sometimes in thought as we cannot exchange many words. I try to make the twilight time my time for thinking of and praying for all the members of our family. First, for all who are suffering much or little from bodily weakness, or need of fuller health, we pray for strength and healing to be poured in, and for spiritual nourishment and strength and joy, the wine of joy to be given, of which the sacramental wine is the symbol. After the invalids we pray for all the brothers and sisters, specially that we may all be prepared gradually and happily for the great change, and helped down the steep last downward paths of life, that those who are to linger to old age may have a happy sojourning in the Land of Beulah. Then we pray for all the young people, asking for all sorts of spiritual and temporal blessings for them, according as we know their needs, and where we do not, commending their wants to Him who sees into their hearts."

The last enemy of Annie's peace was a fear she had of the physical pains of dying. She never spoke of this to those nearest to her, fearing to increase their pain by letting them know of hers, but she confided it to a very dear friend who came to see her constantly, and asked her to pray that the dread might be taken away.

The winter passed, and Annie still lingered. Every day another downward step was taken, until at last she could only be wheeled from her bed to her sitting-room. The latter half of the last chapter of

her book had been written in pencil by Annie
during the winter. It was copied out for her, she
dictating, during this time of weakness, about a
fortnight before the end, when it had become difficult to her to speak more than a few sentences at
a time.

"Let us put it aside for to-day," her amanuensis
said upon one occasion, seeing how much the effort
tried her. "No, no," the hasty reponse came, "let
us work while it is day, the night cometh when no
man can work." It is pleasant to think that she did
persevere that day, and that we have the last sentences
she ever strung together in a tale. No other day
came in which even that slight labour would have
been possible to her; and her pencil writing at that
time it was almost impossible to decipher. Annie
used to sleep for hours at a time upon her couch in
the sitting-room. The room was always made bright
for her by offerings of flowers from near and distant
friends; a little vase of the flowers stood near her couch
once or twice it was filled with snowdrops that had
been transplanted from the garden of the country
rectory where she was born. Her frame was almost
exhausted, but her mind remained perfectly clear, and
her spirits were still bright. She generally awoke
from her long sleeps saying "I have had such a
beautiful dream." Sometimes it would be a dream
of reminiscence that sleep brought, a flower from her
own spring laid upon the death-pillow, and the sight
of it had power to gladden her still. Spiritualists
tell us that the souls of dying people are really taken

whilst the body sleeps, to visit the spheres to which they are going, in order that they may feel at home there when the change comes. That is a pleasant fancy, but one does not need it to feel sure that it was some soothing spiritual influence which made our sleeper awake so joyfully.

Once more Emelia had to leave her friend, to part with her for ever in this world. After she went a cousin of Annie's came to be near her, and remained with her during the last weeks of her life, one whom she had not seen for some years, and to whom she was tenderly attached. One day, on awaking from a long rest, Annie said to her cousin (referring to a book she had just read), "I wonder what new names we shall have, Emily, in the other life," and then she began to name some of her friends according to her idea of their characters. One was to be called "Mother-Sister," and another "Sister-Mother." "And you, Emily," she said, "you must be called 'Lover,' because you love so warmly. And I," she added after a pause, "if I should be found worthy of any name, I should like mine to be 'Sister-Aunt.'" She was thinking of the two strongest affections of her life when she spoke.

The last days came; her brothers and sisters visited her, one by one, as she was able to see them. A week before she died she received the Holy Communion with her sister and her cousin, and the one of her nephews who happened to be with her on that Sunday. The prayer of her heart for weeks had been that she might not be taken until those

who loved her best could bear to let her go; for
herself, she had no pleasure left in this state, and
personally would have liked the time to be shortened.
There was no breath of doubt or fear of any kind
to disturb her then. It seemed as if she only waited
for love to release her. " I am so afraid," she used to
say, " that you love me better than you love Christ,"
for she would fain have seen the Comforter come
into the place that she was soon to leave empty.
On the morning of the 2nd of March, the very day
year on which she had been told of her danger, she
was taken from bed as usual, and laid upon her
couch in the sitting-room, not seeming much weaker
than she had done any day during the last ten days.
She was able to talk to her friends, and admired
some of her favourite shells, that one of her
nephews brought her from the shore. She gave a
slight sketch that day of a little Irish story which
she thought might be written for a children's paper,
" Molly Malony " it was to be called, and was to be
about one of the times of rebellion, when an old
man and a little girl were to be engaged together in
hiding arms for the rebels. It opened in this way :
An old man, employed by the society called " Molly
Malony," very old, and very feeble, and half silly,
is sitting on the side of a hill, repeating over and
over to himself the name of the secret society for
which he has been working. " Molly Malony," he
keeps calling, and at last a little girl runs up to him
and says, " I am Molly Malony" (for that happened
to be her name); " what do you want with me ?"

The old man, interrupted in his dreamy thoughts, takes it into his head that the little maiden is a fairy, come out of Good People's Hollow to help him in the task for which his strength is scarcely sufficient. After a good deal of talking at cross purposes, and after several meetings, a tie of friendship is established between the two, who work together, collecting and hiding arms in the early mornings and late at evening all through the autumn into the winter months. At last, one morning, about Christmas time, the little girl finds her old friend stretched upon the hill-side dying. Then he tells her to do no more work of hiding the arms; he says she is to love Ireland, for that is the true meaning of her name, and for him, he cannot do any more work either, he is going to the land of peace and good will, good will and peace.

The idea of the story seemed to interest her a little, and she gave the sketch of it when it had already become difficult to her to pronounce her words distinctly. The morning and the afternoon passed, and towards evening a change began; Annie asked to be taken to bed again, and said to her attendant: "I am going home soon, Fanny, and I am very happy."

During the night consciousness failed, and she fell into a state of torpor from which she never awoke. Four hours after her spirit passed away, early on the morning of her birthday, the 3rd of March. As she was lying down, the last night, she said to her cousin, "Now I will say a baby hymn," and then she repeated a verse which she had been used to say to the children at the hospital—

> " ' Whether I wake, or whether I sleep,
> I give my soul to Christ to keep,
> Sleep I now, wake I never,
> I give my soul to Christ for ever ; ' "

adding, " Your soul, Emily; yours and mine."

With the words of little children on her lips, and with joy and tenderness in her heart, she was taken home. Home she called that life of which we can form no image. It revealed itself to her by the name that was dearest to her of any name on earth.

THE END

LONDON : R. CLAY, SONS, AND TAYLOR, PRINTERS.